WHAT'S THERE TO THINK ABOUT?

"Dannie," Brant called after her.

Daniella heard him, but she didn't look back. Her plans had gone awry. Brant was asking her for more than she could give. She had lost all trust in the affairs of the heart. How could he put her on the spot like that? she thought while waiting for a cab.

It wasn't long before Brant was beside her. He slipped his arms around Daniella's waist and drew her close.

"I brought you here and I'm taking you home," he said, drawing her close. Slowly, his lips touched hers. Daniella felt her legs weaken as he gathered her closer.

"I need to think, Brant," Daniella said.

"About what, us?" His breath was hot against her lips.

Daniella sank against his muscular chest.

"Yes," she said, trying to find the strength to tear out of his embrace.

Brant caressed Daniella's face with a soft gaze before he lowered his head farther, claiming her lips with a burning kiss that left her swirling and tingling. Without thinking, she returned his kisses freely.

Suddenly, Brant pulled away, and held Daniella at arm's length.

"Let's go."

BOOK YOUR PLACE ON OUR WEBSITE AND MAKE THE ARABESQUE ROMANCE CONNECTION!

We've created a customized website just for our very special Arabesque readers, where you can get the inside scoop on everything that's going on with Arabesque romance novels.

When you come online, you'll have the exciting opportunity to:

- View covers of upcoming books

- Learn about our future publishing schedule (listed by publication month and author)

- Find out when your favorite authors will be visiting a city near you.

- Search for and order backlist books from our line catalog

- Check out author bios and background information

- Send e-mail to your favorite authors

- Join us in weekly chats with authors, readers and other guests

- Get writing guidelines

- AND MUCH MORE!

Visit our website at
http://www.arabesquebooks.com

LOVE BY DESIGN

MARCELLA SANDERS

BET Publications, LLC
www.msbet.com
www.arabesquebooks.com

ARABESQUE BOOKS are published by

BET Publications, LLC
c/o BET BOOKS
One BET Plaza
1900 W Place NE
Washington, D.C. 20018-1211

First Printing: June, 1999
10 9 8 7 6 5 4 3 2 1

Printed in the United States of America

CHAPTER 1

"You're doing *what*?" Daniella Taylor swirled around on her two-inch black pumps and glared at Brant Parker.

"You heard me," Brant said, leaning against the receptionist's desk, returning her empty gaze.

She glanced into his cool, light brown eyes, then lowered her gaze, letting her eyes slip over his muscular physique. Brant Parker wasn't dressed as if he were anyone's boss. His blue pullover shirt strained against his rock-wide chest. His faded jeans hugged his strong, long legs and thighs and his cap was pulled low over his thick brows.

"I thought I heard you say that you couldn't afford to pay two designers to work in the decorators' department, and you're making me your assistant," Daniella said, wishing she had misunderstood her boss. She understood that clients weren't decorating their homes on a whim lately because of the mild recession, but for Brant to demote her in the department was a power play.

"That's the only solution to the problem, Dannie," Brant said. "I've checked and rechecked the accounts. I can't afford to lose money."

Daniella quailed from the exasperation that coursed through her body. She wouldn't allow Brant to take her job. That was all there was to it. She had to fight for what was rightfully hers. Slowly she walked over to the table and poured herself a cup of coffee. As she walked to the table, Daniella caught a glimpse of herself in the mirror. The row of silver snaps on her blue coveralls began just above her cleavage, exposing her cashmered chest. She took a napkin from the stack and blotted her red lips, and carefully sipped the hot coffee.

"Just like that, I get to work with you," Daniella implored. She took another sip of the coffee, then set the cup down. It was summer, too warm for hot drinks, but the need to calm her frazzled nerves was more important. She moved over to the tinted picture window that gave her a clear view of the parking lot. As she looked out at her green Jeep parked beside Brant's white pickup, she saw Brant's six-foot-three reflection through the window behind her.

"Do you have a problem with that?" Brant asked.

Daniella turned to look at him. The coolness in his light brown eyes seemed to have softened, along with the hardness that had lined his mouth earlier.

"Well. . .wouldn't it be better if Beverly worked with you instead?" Daniella suggested, keeping in mind her dislike for drawing residential plans.

"I have looked at every possible angle of this thing

and it's not working, Dannie." Brant rubbed the back of his neck and leaned against the receptionist's desk.

Daniella walked back over to the table where the coffee, strawberries, Brie cheese, and stone-wheat crackers had looked tempting earlier that morning in the reception area. Suddenly, she had lost her appetite when she learned of Brant's decision to make her his assistant.

"Give me and Beverly a chance to at least advertise for new customers," Daniella pleaded with Brant.

"No, I've made up my mind," Brant said.

Not being able to convince Brant not to take the job she loved away from her was almost too much to bear.

"You're not playing fair," Daniella said, determined to control the tremor in her voice. She was already missing her work—gilding, stenciling, upholstering furniture, and just being creative, decorating homes, making them beautiful again.

Brant folded his arms across his chest and gazed at Daniella for a long time. "I'm sorry, Dannie."

"What about the projects I'm working on now?" Daniella asked. She knew for a fact that the work wouldn't be completed until midsummer.

"Don't worry, Beverly will finish it," Brant assured Daniella.

Daniella wasn't sure what irritated her more, the chill that lingered at the edge of Brant's voice or the fact that he wanted her to assist him.

"Brant I hate being tied down to a drawing board, and. . ." she began, when Brant held up his hand stopping her.

"Listen, Dannie, I have a lot of out-of-town assignments and I need someone to travel with me," Brant said.

Daniella groaned. The conversation was getting worse.

"Travel? What's wrong with Tyrone? Is he leaving the company?" Daniella asked, remembering the short romance she and Brant had begun some years ago before company policy forced them apart. Daniella dismissed the memory. She had gotten married 18 months later and only God knew what Brant did afterward.

"No, he wants to spend more time with Beverly and T.J.," Brant replied.

"I can understand him wanting to be with his wife and son," Daniella said. She didn't look at Brant. Her memories of their brief passionate romance saddened her. It reminded her that after her marriage crumbled, she would never love again.

Daniella smacked her coffee cup down on the table as if the action would wipe out the memories of her and Brant's last passionate kiss. Besides that fact, she should have known that arguing with Brant Parker was a waste of time. However, she was willing to wage war with him if necessary.

"I've always made money for the interior design department. The figures from last year alone would be enough to keep us floating until the recession is over," Daniella said, defending her track record. "If you . . ."

"I run my company on facts, Dannie, not ifs, buts, and maybes."

Disgusted, Daniella crossed over to the purple sofa and sat on the edge of the plump cushion.

"Your father would've given me a **chance**," Daniella replied.

"Probably, but he's no longer running this company. I'm in charge here. So, you can work with me or you can resign." Brant was adamant.

Slowly, Daniella twisted a long strand of black hair that had slipped out of her neat bun between her fingers. Panic raced through her at the choice she had to make. She couldn't stop working. She'd just bought a town house, and the money she was awarded from her divorce was in mutual and retirement funds and a few other investments. Daniella bit her bottom lip to keep from arguing with Brant.

"So, when do I start working with you?" Daniella inquired, as the thought of her arguing with disgruntled contractors winged its way across her mind. Usually by the time the homes were remodeled, she didn't want to see them.

"Today is Friday. I expect you in my work area first thing Monday morning," Brant said.

"Monday? I'm supposed to finish decorating a house next week." She patted her chest with her finger. "Me. . .not Beverly," Daniella said.

"Beverly can finish that," Brant stated.

Apprehension sprinted through Daniella as she silently shifted her gaze to Brant's lips. His mouth was as hard and relentless as the final decision he had made concerning her employment. He ran one finger over his thick, black mustache. Brant Parker seemed undisturbed by her reaction, Daniella mused. He appeared content with his position as boss, his masculinity, and his ability to force her to work with him. Daniella swallowed hard. Again, remembering how she had once been attracted to Brant years ago, before she was married to Ray Spencer.

"What are my duties, other than traveling with you?" Daniella asked, knowing well what working with Brant consisted of.

"I'll need you to draw designs for central air and heat vents for projects the company is remodeling," Brant said.

Daniella's arched brows knitted into a frown. *Oh God, I'll be bored stupid,* she thought. It was bad enough that she would have to travel to boring sites and sleep in hotel beds in some lonely city or town. It was almost impossible for her to sleep in strange places. But this was her career and she would sleep.

However, the fact still remained that she would be traveling with Brant Parker who was drop-dead handsome. Being stuck in some town or city alone with him could pose a problem for her. She would be risking smothered flames that had once sparked her heart, hot enough to melt the ice that had carefully preserved her passionate emotions.

Daniella remembered the promise that she had made to herself after her divorce a year ago. She would never involve herself in another serious relationship. The one or two dates she'd had since her divorce had been fun. All heavy breathing and talks of making the relationship serious were excluded from her dating conversation.

Nevertheless, Daniella kept her emotions in check when she was in Brant's presence. It wasn't that he'd ever insinuated that he wanted to date her after her divorce, nor had Brant Parker made any sensual remarks suggesting that he was remotely interested in her. It was the subtle fragrance of his cologne, the light in his eyes. The sound of his smooth voice, and today, past memories had floated across her mind like a ghost on a hot summer night.

Daniella rose from the sofa. It was clear that their meeting was over. She cast a quick glance at Brant, as he lifted the phone's receiver and punched in the digits to whomever he was calling.

Brant is getting on my nerves, Daniella thought, casting him a cool glance and sitting back on the sofa. There had to be a way out of this predicament, she mused. She could simply grab the collar of his pullover and attempt to shake some sense into him. *Naaa,* she thought as she pondered over her decision to get even with her boss for taking the work that she loved away from her. *I can be friendly, at least until I get my old job back,* she thought. On the edge of that thought was a reminder that she couldn't chance becoming too friendly with Brant. She was already attracted to him.

Daniella glanced around the reception area that had once seemed inviting and cheerful. Tall green corn plants rose from large gold buckets in the far corner against the cream-colored walls. The receptionist's desk was a thick, long glass top that sat on two gray oak branches. A picture of a home development encased in a glass frame hung on the wall behind the desk.

While absorbing the features of the room, a dull ache throbbed in Daniella's temples. She fished around in her purse for her sinus prescription. It was no use trying to win two battles in one morning. She had lost the first round with Brant, she wasn't losing the next part of the day to a sinus headache.

Daniella stood and went to pour herself a cup of

water to wash down the pill. As she swallowed the medicine, it dawned on her that for the last couple of years, she had lost many things that she had loved. But losing the right to do what she enjoyed was a cat of a different color. She crushed the paper cup between her fingers, tossed it in the trash basket, ignored Brant, and left the room.

The door to the interior design department was standing open. Daniella leaned against the doorjamb and glanced around the spacious area. The place was like home to her. She had worked long hours in this department, especially on weekends, to keep from going home to face her loneliness. She went over to the table and folded the half yard of red fabric that she had purchased to make a huge pillow. Without thinking, she put the material aside and sat at her work counter.

The interior design department had lacked luster and was painted a mousy brown when Brant's father, Mark, assigned Daniella and Beverly to the department.

Within a short time, the women had added color to the dull room. Daniella suggested that they paint a mural. The ocean she and Beverly designed was surrounded with paint the color of white beach sand. Behind the pink and lavender clouds that laced the early evening sky, strands of a gold sun sank low in the western hemisphere, generating a meditative calmness for anyone who studied the scenery for a while.

Nights when Daniella worked late, the mural served as a source of peace for her. It kept her from focusing on her problems, her nonexistent love life, and her ruined marriage.

Beverly strutted in carrying a straw basket that served as a carrier for a box of assorted doughnuts, the morning's mail, and a memo. Her blue coveralls made a swishing sound as she walked toward Daniella's work counter. Her pecan-brown complexion was clean, flawless, and free of makeup with the exception of a hint of red lipstick.

"Hi," Beverly spoke to Daniella. Her brown eyes sparkled, matching her cheerful smile.

"Morning." Daniella spoke dryly, releasing all considerations of her dull life.

"You're here early," Beverly said, dropping the mail and memo on Daniella's work counter. Her black blunt haircut bounced above her shoulders as she flopped down on the sofa.

"Yeah," Daniella said, tapping her short French-manicured nails against the counter's top.

"What's up?" Beverly asked, as she carefully opened the box of doughnuts.

"After today, I'll be assisting Brant." Daniella laced her fingers together and gave them an annoying pop.

"Girl, don't play with me," Beverly said, scooting closer to the edge of the sofa.

"I'm serious. According to him, we're losing money," Daniella replied, informing her girlfriend of Brant's final decision.

"And who's supposed to work with me?" Beverly stood up. Her red lips pursing with slight irritation.

Daniella shrugged, considering Beverly's question. "Beats the heck out of me." She hadn't thought to ask Brant how Beverly was going to handle the projects alone.

"Where is that tramp?" Beverly asked.

"Tramp?" Daniella chuckled.

"I would like to call him that to his face, but I need my job," Beverly said, turning around to face Daniella. "Is Brant is his office?"

"I left him up front making phone calls," Daniella said, watching while Beverly hurried from the room to find Brant.

Daniella unlocked her fingers and reached for the mail and the memo. She unfolded the memo and read the announcement for the company's annual picnic. The memo informed Parker's Art employees that this year the picnic was canceled. Daniella rolled the memo into a neat ball and dropped the paper in the trash beside her counter. She assumed that this was another one of Brant's money-saving tactics.

Some boss he turned out to be, Daniella mused, allowing her mind to spin back to the last picnic she had attended before she resigned, got married, and moved to Florida.

It was the first time that she'd really given Brant Parker a second thought. For one reason, Brant's father had a company policy: Employees weren't allowed to date. Mark Parker had determined that romancing on the job posed too many problems. But at the company's picnic, Brant and Daniella had spent the entire day together. As soon as she arrived at the lake, Daniella headed for one of the many chaise lounges that sat under a row of pitch pines near the lake. She unpacked her sunscreen and novel that she'd been reading the night before. But instead of reading, Daniella looked out at the blue lake when she noticed Brant swimming toward her. Seconds later, he was standing over the chaise lounge next to her, drying himself with a towel. As Daniella stole glances at him. She noticed his strong, long legs;

narrow hips; and a chest that seemed as hard as stone. When Daniella thought that Brant had sensed her looking at him, she quickly turned her attention back to her book. Brant sat down on the lounge next to her and began to talk about their work and the book she was reading. Brant had laughed when she told him that her book was a romance. When Daniella wanted to know what was funny, Brant simply told her that he preferred reading adventures.

As Brant and Daniella talked, she noticed his face— his strong cleft chin and hard mouth that she imagined would soften with a kiss. His black mustache was thick and neat. Before Daniella could look away, Brant looked at her. His light brown eyes were soft and warm. His honey complexion was smooth. When he asked her to walk with him, she agreed.

They walked along the edge of the woods in silence until Brant came to a house. He told her that one day he wanted to own a home near that lake. Daniella wasn't sure why Brant was discussing his dreams and plans with her as if they were old friends, but she had listened. When they turned down the path that led them back to the others, Brant slipped his arms around her waist. He reminded her of his father's old-fashioned rule, but despite that fact, Brant asked Daniella if she would be his friend. Daniella didn't agree to go out with Brant. Her concern was that they would be breaking company rules. Brant assured Daniella that in the future he would own Parker's Art and the dating rule was the first one he intended to discard.

They spent the day together, swimming, eating, dancing, and having fun. At the end of the day, Daniella and Brant walked to her car. After he had helped her pack away the chaise lounge in the car's trunk, he gathered her in his arms and brushed her lips lightly with his, leaving Daniella almost breathless. When Brant moved away from her, he had smiled, promising to see her the next evening.

Saturday night, Daniella and Brant went to a 1960's dance in the park. They did the Peppermint Twist and the Night Train. They watched the older couples move to the oldie goldies. When they had figured out the steps, Daniella and Brant would join the others on the makeshift dance floor.

When the evening was over, Brant drove Daniella to her apartment. They didn't talk much as Brant drove around the winding roads and hills. As they drove past the horse farm, Brant broke the silence, asking Daniella if she could ride. When Daniella said she had only ridden a horse twice, Brant promised her that they would go riding the next weekend. She never remembered having so much fun. Finally, Brant turned off the winding road that led to Daniella's apartment. Soft lights lit several of the two-story apartment buildings. Brant pulled up to the curb in front of Daniella's building. He got out and walked around to open her door. Like a gentleman, he walked her to her door and waited while she unlocked it. When she had dropped her keys inside her purse, Brant pulled her to him and kissed her, planting little kisses on her lips and finally offering long, deep, and passionate kisses. As much as Daniella wanted to, she decided that being involved with Brant could cost her her employment. So she promised herself that night after his kisses that she would wait.

Daniella didn't have to wait long. Monday morning, Mark Parker called a staff meeting. He wasn't sure if the rumor were true. However, he was prepared to fire the couple that took it upon themselves to defy his policy. Mark made it clear that Brant was not an exception.

Daniella avoided Brant after that and returned only one of his phone calls. She reminded him of Parker's Art no-dating policy. She would not have a concealed relationship.

Six months after her fling with Brant, Daniella met Ray Spencer. A year later, Daniella announced her engagement in the staff meeting. She didn't understand why Brant seemed distressed. He knew the rules.

Without further consideration of Brant's heart-rending expression, Daniella married Ray and moved to Fort Lauderdale, Florida.

Two years later, Daniella was divorced. She returned to New Jersey. Mark Parker gave Daniella her job back assigning her to work with Beverly in the interior design department to boot.

Daniella let her thoughts return from the past. Her life was peaceful now. She was home to stay. She loved Forest, New Jersey. A quiet town that sat adjacent to the north of Philadephia and was fifteen minutes from New York. The bedroom community that she lived in with its tudor-roofed town houses was fairly new. The park that sat across the street from her town house was lined with pitch pines, red oak, and silver maples. A pond sat in the center of the park where ducks swam and where black rails flew down from their perches and drank the pond's cool water.

Just as Daniella tossed the memo into the garbage, the phone rang. "Parker's Art," Daniella said.

"Dannie, how are you?" Annie Mae Taylor asked her daughter.

"Hi, Mother," Daniella said. "I'm fine. Is everything all right with you and daddy?" Daniella asked, surprised that her mother had called her early in the morning from the Bahamas.

"Sure. I called you last night. I figured you were out so I decided to call you at work," Annie Mae said. "Are you still working late hours?"

"Sometimes," Daniella said, not wanting to worry her mother. She had been receiving anonymous phone calls at night and had turned the ringer on her phone off. "Are you and daddy enjoying your vacation?"

"Yes we are. Your daddy sends his love."

"Where is he?" Daniella asked wanting to speak to her father.

"He went fishing early this morning," Annie Mae said, laughing.

"Sounds like he's having fun."

"He is. Listen Dannie, will you do me a favor and purchase our tickets for the Women's Charity Ball?" Annie Mae asked.

"Sure, Mother."

"Thank you. Jake and I will see you soon. We wish you were here."

Daniella said goodbye to her mother and shook her head. The last place she wanted to be in the middle of June was the Bahamas.

She opened the letter from the community center. The executive director was thanking her for volunteering her time with the dance class. Could she volunteer two nights a week instead of one?

Daniella made a face. *Why not,* she thought. She

didn't have a social life. One night a week she and
Beverly went to the Café with a few other designers
from work for dinner, dancing, drinks and mostly
gossip. Saturday afternoon, she usually went to the
video store for a good movie to watch Saturday night
and Sunday if she didn't oversleep, she went to
church. The rest of her day was spent shopping or
watching a good game on television. *Yes, I'll volunteer
two nights a week,* Daniella decided. *It'll give me something to do when I'm not on the road with Brant.*

The door popped open and Beverly stormed in.
She flopped down on the sofa this time with much
more gusto than before. Her pecan-brown skin
seemed to have darkened with frustration.

"Uh, uh, uh," Beverly groaned. Digging into the
doughnut box, she took out a honey-glazed and
motioned for Daniella to join her.

"Do you think if we strangle Brant, it'll help our
case?" Daniella asked, going over, sitting next to Beverly. She took out a chocolate-coated doughnut and
licked the sweet coating, closing her eyes, as she nib-
bled the edges.

"Strangling him is much too good. I think you
should seduce him," Beverly said, giggling.

"Yeah, right." Daniella cast her girlfriend a cool
glance.

"It would serve him right. Everybody around here
knows he's crazy about you, and mad because you
wouldn't give him the time of day," Beverly said.

"You mean everybody knows that except me," Daniella replied.

"Well I guess it's true, the woman is the last to
know." Beverly gave Daniella an impish smile.

"Girl, please," Daniella said. Leading Brant down

a primrose path was the last thing she intended to add to her things to do list. "I don't know why you asked him to hire another designer. I could've told you that you were wasting your time," Daniella said.

"I know, but it felt good to yell at him," Beverly said.

Daniella smiled. She raised her legs and rested them on the coffee table. "Ummm hmmm, I'll stop by and visit every chance I get and we'll still do lunch and catch up on all the latest gossip."

Beverly drew in a deep breath and closed her eyes. For a moment she seemed to have been thinking. "Apparently, Brant is trying to make you quit. What do you think?" Beverly took another doughnut from the box.

"I don't know." Daniella bit into the doughnut and chewed slowly. "I think he has let his position as boss go to his head."

"So go after him with vigor," Beverly said, giggling.

"And have his girlfriend, Glenda, hot on my trail?" Daniella asked. "Uh-uh, not me."

"I heard that Brant wasn't seeing her anymore," Beverly said in a slow, even voice.

"Gossip," Daniella stated firmly. I saw Glenda switching around her yesterday.

"So?" Beverly said. "Seduce him anyway, he's not a married man, you know." Beverly looked at Daniella. "That way, you can sweet-talk him and soon, we'll be working together again."

The expression on Beverly's face and the tone of her voice seemed serious to Daniella. "I'm willing to do just about anything to keep from drawing another design. But seducing Brant is not one of them, Beverly. Sometimes, you have the most hair-brained ideas," Daniella said, thinking how, if she was silly enough to throw herself on the man, she wouldn't have space in her heart to love him anyway.

"Well, it was a suggestion." Beverly smothered another giggle.

The phone rang. Daniella got up and answered it.

"Dannie, here," she answered, frowning as the caller's loud breathing pulsated against her eardrums. The rollicking sound of the caller's nasal breathing produced goose bumps on her skin. Sheer black fear coursed through her insides.

"Who is this?" Daniella asked. Although, she figured it was the same man that had called at the beginning of the week.

"Slut," the smothered voice said.

"Go play in traffic!" Daniella slammed the receiver in its cradle.

"Dannie, was that the same creep that called you a few days ago?" Beverly asked.

"Yes, and the next time I see a sign in someone's yard advertising antiques, remind me to keep driving." Daniella checked her watch. "I have this habit of giving out my business cards."

"I'll darn sure do it, because that man is a creep," Beverly said.

Daniella had about ten minutes to drive to the Carriage Place and get started on her beautification project. She walked over to her work counter and picked up her purse.

"I want to get as much work finished on this house by the end of the week as I can," Daniella said, putting the letters that she had received earlier into her purse. "I'll give you all the details on the project later, since

Brant wants you to complete it.'' She walked toward the door.

"Okay, are you going to Omar's for lunch?" Beverly asked.

"I might," Daniella said. Going to Omar's for lunch meant running into Brant. The less she saw of Brant Parker today, the better. There was no telling what she might do or say to him if she found herself in his presence. It was bad enough that she was forced to work in close quarters with the arrogant, bossy, good-looking hunk. *Lord, what am I going to do?* With that question quietly directed to the Supreme Being, Daniella stepped out into the corridor.

If Brant Parker thought she was going to roll over and play dead, while he took the job that she loved away from her, he had better think again.

Daniella was a fighter. When she was a young girl, she didn't mind popping a boy her age with a left-right hook if she had to defend herself.

Today, she detested violence. She went after her enemy's jugular in a quiet, subtle way once she learned his weakness.

CHAPTER 2

In his office, Brant sat at the drawing board rehashing the meeting he'd had with Daniella that morning. He leaned back in the chair and planted his hands on his narrow hips.

As Brant recalled his meeting with Daniella, he remembered how her ebony eyes seemed to have lost their sparkle when he mentioned his decision to have her work with him. Brant tapped his forefinger against his chin. *I did the right thing,* he mused, considering his decision to change Daniella's position. Tyrone wanted to work closer to home since he and Beverly were parents now. And why should he hire an assistant when Daniella had all the experience and job requirements. Brant got up, pushed his hands down in the top of his jeans' pockets and walked over to the window. As he looked out at a bed of red and yellow tulips circling the stone water fountain, he thought of Daniella again. The flowers' beauty reminded him of her. But for some reason Daniella had changed over the years. She was more determined, she seemed stronger and more stubborn than he remembered. Daniella was strong mentally, like a mountain standing in the center of an ocean.

But this morning he had been successful in the quest of making his point. He no longer needed two employees for the interior design department. And then there was the budget to think about. When his father retired and gave him Parker's Art, Mark made Brant promise that he would maintain the business as usual. Brant had agreed. He was a man that kept his promises and he would keep the promise he'd made to his daddy.

He wasn't proud that he had taken Daniella away from the job she loved. But unlike his best friend, Tyrone, Daniella was single, she didn't have a child, and she was free to travel.

Brant went back to his drawing board. He covered his face with his hands and rubbed his eyes. He was tired. For the last few weeks he had worked twelve and fifteen hours a day. Yes, he needed Daniella whether she liked it or not. Brant picked up the yellow pencil and attempted to work on plan 400 again. His thoughts returned to Daniella.

Daniella seemed shocked when he told her that she would travel with him. He tried to dismiss the thought, because he wasn't sure how he was going to handle being alone with her for long periods of time. He was well aware of her physical and mental attributes. He had watched her this morning as she nervously twisted the ends of her hair. How her mouth had puckered into a pout and then he allowed his mind to swing back to the day of the company's picnic years ago when he had kissed Daniella. Her lips had tasted like the cherry lipstick she wore. Brant thought it was best that he didn't think of Daniella. He'd had his chance to love her once, but he chose Parker's Art. His father had promised him the business once he retired. When Mark learned that he was dating one of the employees, he called a meeting and threatened to fire him. Brant made a choice and it wasn't Daniella. When Daniella announced that she was engaged, it was like she had reached into his chest and snatched out his heart. Since she had been back in town, Daniella hadn't seemed to notice him. So he assumed that she was still in love with her ex-husband.

Brant went back to his half-finished plan. If he didn't complete plan 400 today, he knew he would work late tonight. Once again, his mind went back to Daniella. This morning he had wanted to touch her, to comfort her. But he knew better than to make that kind of move.

Brant gave up on working on plan 400, he decided that he would complete it later that day. By then he was sure his thoughts of Daniella would be resting in the back of his mind.

He went to his desk. The leather-bound appointment book on his desk was opened to the things to Do list for next week's agenda. He had a Business Council meeting Monday morning. He planned to take Daniella with him and introduce her to the members. That way, when he was unable to attend meetings, Daniella could represent Parker's Art. He closed the appointment book, and put away the plan he was working on. Brant took his cap from his office closet, before heading out to find Tyrone so they could go to lunch.

Just as Brant stepped out into the corridor, he heard the receptionist's voice come across the intercom, calling the security guard. He took off down the hallway in a trot as the receptionist's soft voice floated through the speakers.

As Brant jogged passed Tyrone's office door, Tyrone walked out of his office and stood in the hallway. His tall, dark, muscular frame towered over a young lady who had run out of an office to no doubt see who security was removing from the building.

"What is going on?" Tyrone asked Brant as they headed toward the front of the building.

"I don't know," Brant said, sliding into the reception area, almost knocking Glenda to the floor.

"Glenda what are you doing here?" Brant asked.

Glenda brushed an artificial auburn strand back from her forehead. She moved closer to Brant and looked up at him through dark, slanted eyes. She placed her manicured hands on his chest and smiled seductively. "What do you think?"

Brant took a couple of steps back. "I don't know, you tell me." He glared at the woman who insisted that no matter what happened, she wasn't going to stop loving him.

"I stopped by to take you to lunch and this . . . this woman barricaded the door and wouldn't let me see you," Glenda said, pointing a long red nail at the receptionist who had kept her from barging into Brant's office.

Brant turned around. Tyrone stood near the desk, his arms folded across his chest watching Brant.

Brant inclined his head, keeping his voice low, so

that Tyrone and the others wouldn't hear him speaking to Glenda. As Brant spoke to her, he avoided eye contact with the low-cut orange dress she was wearing.

"I want you to leave the building now," he whispered, grinding the words between his teeth.

Glenda planted one hand on her hip. "Brant, why are you being stubborn. You know it'll never be over between us." Glenda said, her voice rising a notch.

Brant glanced around again, several of his employees were making trips to the receptionist's desk to pick up one thing or another. He was sure they were all being nosy.

"Glenda, don't make another scene in this room," Brant said in a low, icy tone.

"I need to talk to you," Glenda said, lowering her voice. "And I left a gift for you with the receptionist."

"A gift?" Brant asked, glancing around the room again as if he was expecting to see a huge box sitting in the corner. This was Glenda he was dealing with and anything she did wasn't a surprise to him.

"I have been leaving messages on your voice mail all week and you haven't returned one of my calls," Glenda said.

"Glenda, listen to me . . ." Brant started, but she continued to speak.

"No. I went by your place yesterday and that maid of yours wouldn't open the door."

Brant clamped his mouth shut to keep from yelling at her. Glenda was a persistent woman. He had stayed in control of his anger the three months since he had resolved his relationship with her. He would not allow her to lure him into losing his cool in the presence of his staff.

"Karla was following my orders," Brant said, taking

Glenda's elbow, leading her toward the entrance as Daniella walked into the reception area. She gave him a disapproving look as if he was personally responsible for the disturbance Glenda had started. And splintering on the edge of that thought was the fact that Daniella probably thought he and Glenda were having a lover's quarrel.

Brant cursed under his breath, as he gestured for the security guard.

"I bought your birthday gift almost three months ago, Brant. You could at least take it," Glenda said, casting a brief glance at Daniella.

Embarrassed at the scene Glenda had caused, Brant dismissed the guard and walked Glenda to her car.

It was a good thing he considered himself a gentleman, Brant thought as he opened her car door and waited for her to get in. Mark and Clara had raised him and his brother, Nick, to respect women. Glenda knows this, Brant thought. But she seemed to think his good manners were a sign of weakness.

After one of her tantrums, Brant usually ended up at her house that night for dinner and a romp between the sheets. Things had changed. He was through with Glenda.

"When are you coming over?" Glenda asked as she slid behind the wheel of her BMW.

"We'll talk," Brant said to her, planning to return the gift the first chance he got.

Brant walked over and leaned against the hood of his pickup. He watched as Glenda burned rubber driving out of the parking lot. He'd had it with Glenda's games. The only thing left to do, was to come right out and tell her to leave him alone. He hadn't figured out how he was going to tell her to stay out of his life without hurting her feelings, but if push came to shove, he could do that too.

"Hey Brant, man let's roll up out of here." Tyrone's voice drew Brant out of his daze. He wiped the perspiration from his face with the back of his hand, disalarmed his truck, and climbed behind the wheel.

Tyrone climbed in beside Brant. "Are you all right?" Tyrone asked Brant.

"I'm cool," Brant said to his longtime friend. While turning the key in the ignition, he gave Tyrone a side glance. He figured Tyrone was thinking about his problem with Glenda. "I don't want to hear it."

"Brant, Glenda has a serious problem," Tyrone said.

"You think I don't know?" Brant asked as he backed out of the parking space.

"Why don't you tell her to leave you alone and mean it?" Tyrone said.

"I can't count the times that I've done that, man," Brant said.

Tyrone reached into his shirt pocket and pulled out a long, slim black velvet box and handed it to Brant.

"The receptionist asked me to give this to you," Tyrone said.

"Put it in the glove compartment," Brant said, without looking at the gift.

Tyrone frowned, as he put the gift in the glove compartment.

"See, Tyrone this is what I'm talking about. Glenda thinks that stuff like that gift is going to bring us back together." Brant drove out onto the street and out into the lunch-hour traffic.

"Brant you need to find yourself a woman, get married, and settle down," Tyrone said. "I'm happy."

"I don't have time to find a wife, Ty."

Tyrone shrugged. "Maybe you don't have to look."

Brant shot Tyrone a quick glance. "We're eating at Omar's, right?" Brant changed the subject.

"Yeah."

As they rode in silence, Brant allowed his thoughts to waver. What did Tyrone mean by that statement, "Maybe you don't have to look." He had been ambivalent about marriage for years. Brant's grip tightened on the steering wheel, recalling how close he'd come to marrying Glenda. A month before his birthday in April, Glenda came to him with the oldest trick in the book. Over dinner one night, she happily announced that she was pregnant. Brant had believed her until the day he stopped by her dress and gown boutique. When he didn't see Glenda in the store, he went to her office. Her opened purse sat on the desk. Out of curiosity Brant had cast a brief glance inside the purse when he noticed a new pack of birth-control pills.

Glenda had lied to him and Brant hated liars, especially when it was intended to trap him. He had left her. Glenda had asked for his forgiveness, showered him with expensive gifts, waited in the parking lot for him to leave work, and called him at his home in the middle of the night. *He'd had enough*, Brant mused, pulling into Omar's parking lot.

While they waited for a table, Brant looked around the dining room. On the walls were photos of famous movie stars, heavyweight boxers and their winning boxing gloves, baseball bats, and black-and-white snapshots of the players. Brant moved farther into the restaurant and saw Daniella and Beverly sitting at a table near the window.

Brant and Tyrone joined the women at their table. While Tyrone pulled back a chair and sat next to his wife, Brant stood for a moment gazing at Daniella.

"Ladies," Brant spoke, still looking at Daniella as she speared a cherry tomato and put it in her mouth. When she'd finished eating it, she glanced at Brant.

"What?" Daniella asked Brant, exchanging glances with him.

"Nothing," Brant said, pulling out a chair and sitting across from her. "You don't mind if I join you, do you?" he asked, eyeing her carefully.

"Do I have a choice?" Daniella asked, locking her gaze with his.

"What if I told you no," Brant said, nodding his head to the waiter who had finished serving a couple at the table across from them, letting him know that he was ready to order.

"Then why did you ask," Daniella said, lifting her water glass to her lips, taking a sip.

She's mad at me, Brant thought as he watched Daniella's lips pucker into a stubborn pout.

"Look, Dannie, I know you're upset about the changes taking place at work. But if it's any consolation, I'll buy you lunch," Brant offered, hoping she would forgive him for forcing her to work with him.

"First of all, I can buy my own lunch," Daniella replied.

"It's a peace offering," Brant insisted, turning his attention to the waiter who had taken Tyrone's order and was waiting for Brant.

He ordered a Reuben sandwich and a bottle of seltzer, before leaning back in his chair, giving Dan-

iella his undivided attention. "Now where were we?"
Brant asked Daniella.

"Making peace with me is going to cost you more
than a lousy lunch, so keep your money," Daniella
said.

"You don't have to be so mean about it," Brant
said, half-grinning. He was willing to pay whatever
price the lovely Miss Taylor had in mind if it made
her happy.

Daniella dropped her fork on her plate and for the
first time since Brant had sat across from her, she
gave him her undivided attention.

"I can't stand a man that thinks he can buy a
woman." Daniella glared at him.

Brant looked at Daniella for a long time. Her ebony
eyes seemed to have darkened with anger. "If I
offended you, I'm sorry," Brant said, meaning it.

"Forget it," Daniella picked up her fork, finishing
off her garden salad.

Brant leaned back in his chair and waited for his
sandwich. Off and on, he stole glances at Daniella,
while listening to bits and pieces of Tyrone and Beverly's conversation.

"Tyrone, T.J. will be three years old on his birthday," Beverly reminded her husband.

"So."

"T.J. is too young to go camping with you," Brant
overheard Beverly saying.

"Baby, T.J. needs to learn to do boy stuff," Tyrone
said to Beverly.

"Tyrone, you listen and listen good. My baby is not
leaving that house."

Brant stole another gaze at Daniella while Beverly

and Tyrone discussed little Tyrone Junior's camping adventures. He wondered if she wanted children.

The waiter set Tyrone and Brant's food before them.

"Enjoy your lunch," the waiter said to the guys.

Brant nodded to the waiter and bit into the Reuben, noticing that Daniella had finished her lunch, and was taking money from her purse to pay her bill.

"Are you sure you don't want me to treat you to lunch?" Brant looked up from his sandwich, reaching in his pocket for his wallet.

"No." Daniella looked around for the waiter to bring her the check.

Brant straightened in his chair and went back to his lunch. He had to find a way to make Daniella realize that his decision was business. But then he figured she knew that. Maybe Daniella didn't like him.

James Amour sat two tables behind Brant, Daniella, Tyrone, and Beverly. He stared at Daniella and Brant through deep, dark hooded eyes. James turned his attention back to the warm pea soup he had ordered and began to eat. While he ate, the nagging idea that he'd played with days ago floundered across his mind again when he realized that it was Brant Parker sitting with Daniella and the others.

James knew that Brant Parker owned Parker's Art from listening to Brant and his buddy's conversations in the gym's locker room where he had started working two weeks after he arrived in Forest, New Jersey. James also knew that Parker's Art wasn't just architects, but builders and carpenters as well. Since he never got his carpenter's license, James wondered if Brant would hire him as a handyman. He could use the money. Besides, being employed at Parker's Art would work into his plans. James dipped the spoon back into the pea soup and lifted it to his mouth, careful not to spill food on his thick, black beard.

James swallowed and slowly lifted his dark eyes to give Daniella another icy glare. He turned his attention back to his plan, which consisted of becoming gainfully employed preferably at Parker's Art. He would pay his debts and move to another country. James wiped his mouth with his napkin and then turned to gaze blankly out the window.

His job at the gym paid minimum wage. He couldn't afford to get a haircut, so he wore a ponytail. He couldn't shave because disposable razors irritated his skin. It was a shame that he couldn't afford an electric shaver. Once in his life, he had grown accustomed to the finer things life had to offer. His life had deteriorated over the years and he couldn't afford to give the waiter a decent tip. He reached inside his pants' pocket and took out four quarters and laid them on the table. He could hardly afford the soup. But the day-old fried ham and rubbery eggs he'd eaten for breakfast hadn't settled on his stomach right. James gazed at the back of Brant's head. He got up and started toward the table where Brant and the others were sitting. He changed his mind. He would talk to Brant later. James Amour made an about-face and walked out. His dreams were about to materialize.

CHAPTER 3

Six-thirty Monday morning, Daniella rolled out of bed and made a beeline for the bathroom, willfully masterminding a plan to wage war on Brant Parker. She could quit her job. No, that was too easy and besides Brant would probably like that. Or, she could go ahead and seduce him. Brant would probably like that, too, she mused.

Still uncertain of the plan she'd come up with to make Brant her friend in order to return to her interior designing job, Daniella twisted the shower's nozzle to warm and let spindrifts of water splash against her.

Daniella closed her eyes, shutting out threads of yellow sunrays that shone through her bathroom window, and dismissed all her thoughts of Brant. She couldn't forget Brant. He wanted her to greet strangers and introduce herself too early in the morning at a Business Council meeting she'd rather not attend. The only thing Daniella Taylor wanted was to clasp her palm around a cool Cappuccino Blast.

I've got it, Daniella thought, lathering herself with shower gel. *I'll make Brant my pal.* The only problem with that idea was that she didn't have a clue as to how she was going to pull it off since Brant didn't seem to like her much lately.

Daniella stood under the water, allowing it to splash the suds off her. She reached for the pink plush towel and stepped out.

As she massaged lotion all over herself, the plan to make Brant her pal didn't seem like such a bad idea. She didn't have a thing to lose. Daniella set the lotion bottle on the vanity and sprinkled powder all over herself, then dabbed on her favorite perfume.

The nerve of Brant, Daniella fumed as she darted into her closet and took a white calf-length suit off the rack. He was literally controlling her life. It seemed that the last few years her life had been controlled by a man. No, she wouldn't allow Brant to take the work she loved away from her, Daniella decided.

With that thought safely resting in the back of her mind, Daniella dressed in her white suit and matching heels, and went downstairs, through the kitchen, and to the garage. She got into her Jeep and drove to the hotel.

Several blocks later, Daniella parked in Howard Johnson's parking lot and walked into the lobby. She wasn't surprised when she saw Brant casually chatting with the registration clerk.

For a couple of painstaking moments, Daniella gazed at the man who had rearranged her career. In the place of working long hours on weekend nights, planning to beautify a client's residence, she would probably be in some strange, lonely town with him.

Thanks a lot Brant, Daniella mused, shifting her gaze to the back of Brant's head, gradually allowing her gaze to travel over his tan suit jacket and trousers, on down to his brown wingtips. It wasn't often that Daniella saw Brant in a suit. She was surprised at the unwelcomed fluttering around her heart when Brant turned and looked at her. It was as if he had looked into her soul and read her thoughts.

Get a grip, Dannie, she told herself. *That's how you got in trouble the last time. When are you going to learn that good-looking men spell t-r-o-u-b-l-e.*

At the same time Daniella dwelled on that sound advice, an unexpected warmth coiled through her. Daniella walked up to Brant.

"What're you doing here?" Daniella asked, frustrated at herself for secretly admiring her boss.

Brant took a few steps forward and stopped in front of her.

"I'll have to introduce you to the council members. Let's go in and get breakfast before the meeting starts," Brant said, touching his hand to Daniella's waist, guiding her toward the conference room.

"I could've introduced myself, given the members business cards, and saved you the trip," Daniella replied, glaring into Brant's light brown eyes.

"Dannie did anyone ever tell you that you're not supposed to glare at your boss?"

Daniella shrugged. "So sue me."

Brant chuckled under his breath. "Come on," he said, walking toward the conference room. Brant stopped to talk to a man he knew that owned a coffee and bottled water company. After Brant gave the man a business card and asked him to call his secretary, so they could discuss the monthly cost of a spring water machine and the latest coffee flavors, the man invited Brant to meet him at a billiards hall across town for a game of pool.

Hmmm, Daniella mused, standing next to Brant listening to the conversation, toying with the idea of asking Brant to shoot a game of pool with her. She had played the game for years. It just might be another way to get on his good side.

As she tinkered with the idea of getting into Brant's good graces, she inhaled his invigorating cologne. Brant's pleasing scent brought to mind how much she loved a man that smelled good. She dismissed the thought and moved away from Brant. Standing too close to him was affecting her common sense.

Before Daniella moved toward the business council's meeting room, she glanced over her shoulder at Brant. He had all the qualifications a woman looked for in a good man. He was a no-nonsense kind of guy. He was comfortable with his success, and tailing those considerations, came the thought that Mr. Brant Parker was just as handsome as he could be. If she was in a position to have an *affair de coeur,* it would certainly be with him.

It almost made Daniella shudder to think that she was passionately admiring Brant again. Looks could be deceiving. She recalled how she had fallen for Ray Spencer because of his appearance and attitude. After tangling her emotions with Ray for a few years, Daniella learned that it wasn't safe to assume. She knew Brant was arrogant. She was sure he was also hard-headed and stubborn to boot. Daniella walked inside the room, leaving Brant to his conversation.

The scent of fresh fruit intermingled with the smell of sausage, hash browns, French toast, coffee, and bacon.

Several men and women dressed in business suits sat at round tables covered with white linen tablecloths, engaged in conversation as they ate breakfast or simply sipped coffee. Every once in a while the sound of soft laughter erupted from the business owners.

Attending this meeting might not be the worst thing that could happen, Daniella realized, thinking how relaxed the members appeared.

Just when Daniella reached the breakfast bar, she felt a hand on her waist. Daniella turned around to confront the person intruding on her space.

"Why didn't you wait for me?" Brant removed his hand from Daniella's waist.

"You seemed in control of the conversation." Daniella placed a couple of orange and melon slices and a banana on her plate.

"I needed you with me," Brant said.

Daniella ignored Brant's comment. It was unsuitable to get into a verbal fight with him at the breakfast bar. She watched Brant while he piled his plate with grits, eggs, sausage, and several strips of bacon.

"And you intend to eat all of that food," Daniella said as they walked to the table, joining a beautician, an aesthetician, and a Realtor.

"I like to eat, Dannie." Brant set his plate on the table and pulled back a chair for her.

"I think you're just plain greedy," Daniella said, glancing at the chair and then at Brant, recalling how when she and Ray were dating, he used all of his male charms and manners on her. It was too bad Ray Spencer's manners had been fake.

"Whatever," Brant said, exchanging glances with Daniella. "But will you please sit down."

Because of Ray, Daniella hated for men to do anything for her and that included helping her get seated at a table. Under the circumstances, she decided to sit. Later, Daniella intended to express her opinion to Brant Parker on phony male etiquette.

She spread the white linen napkin in her lap and pulled herself closer to the table.

"Good morning," Daniella spoke to the members at the table and introduced herself.

"Hi, Coleen Jones." Coleen took a business card from the stack that sat next to her coffee cup. She gave one to Daniella. "Bob and Clip Salon, I would love to do business with you." She smiled. Her burnt-orange lipstick seemed to fuse her tawny complexion. Her short black spiral curls were neat and glossy. Coleen reached into her black suit jacket and took out a few more cards to add to her diminishing stack.

Monique McRay set her coffee cup down and smiled. Her smile was equally as bright as Coleen's. She gracefully leaned forward and tucked a long, curly jet-black strand behind her ear, exposing a diamond earring. Her red lips matched her short red nails and cashmere complexion.

"Monique McRay," she said, "owner of Shagreen." Monique lifted a card from her stack and held one out to Daniella. "It's nice to have you join us."

· "Thanks," Daniella said, taking the expensive white business card that had *Shagreen* scribbled in gold letters. While she was reading the card, she noticed that Brant and the man at the table were discussing property.

"How are you?" George LeMann said to Daniella. "I'm George LeMann. LeMann Brokerage," George said, grinning and showing a set of pearl-white teeth. He stood, drawing his tall frame from the chair, walking around the table to shake Daniella's hand. He reached into his suit pocket and gave Daniella a card. Daniella had heard good things about George LeMann's real-estate business, but this was the first time she'd met him. He was the color of chocolate and his head was shaven clean.

"Hi," Daniella said, remembering when she was in the market for her town house she had considered LeMann Brokerage to work with her.

"Ah, Brant was telling me that you're his assistant."

"Yes", Daniella said, giving Brant a side glance.

"Well. Welcome to our meeting," George said and continued his conversation with Brant while they ate.

The only business cards Daniella had were the ones from the interior design department. She glanced at Brant before exchanging her business card with the entrepreneurs.

"You're just the person I need," Coleen said. "George sold me a house a few weeks ago and girl I don't have the first clue on how to make the inside look good."

Daniella gave Brant a side glance, resenting the fact that he had taken the one thing that she loved to do away from her.

"I can't take the job, but I'll give your card to another designer at Parker's Art." Daniella smiled, as she spoke to the beautician. Her name is Beverly and I'll ask her to give you a call."

"And if you need any hair services, Coleen will be happy to assist you," George said, giving Coleen a playful wink.

"Oh, shut up, George," Coleen said, pulling at a springy spiral curl that stopped just below her nape area. "I was trying out a new hairstyle and. . ." her cheerful voice faded when Brant and George laughed.

"I think it's a nice hairstyle," Daniella added, more annoyed at Brant for chuckling than she was at George.

"Daniella you'll soon get used to this crowd. They're excellent businesspeople, but they don't have one ounce of sense when it comes to fashion," Monique said, taking a stack of ten-percent discount flyers from her briefcase to give to the members.

"I agree," Daniella said, laughing and looking at Brant. But Brant Parker didn't fit in that category, he had style.

"Don't pay George any attention, he's just jealous because he doesn't have hair to comb, let alone style," Coleen replied. She looked at George over the rim of her coffee cup.

While the members at the table joked about George's lack of hair, Daniella gazed at Brant's thick, ebony waves for a second or two. Brant Parker would never have to worry about losing his hair, she decided.

"You guys are behind the times. Don't you know bald is in?" George swept his hand over his clean head.

Brant chuckled softly.

The sound of Brant's laughter floated over Daniella. If she didn't know better, she would've been bamboozled into thinking that the fluttering in her chest was the sign of being more attracted to Brant than she should be. Daniella sat quietly sipping her orange juice. It was as if the cold liquid would wash away any warm feelings she was having for Brant.

The president of the council stepped up to the mahogany rostrum. He was a man of average height who seemed to be in his late fifties. His light brown hair grayed at the temples. He cleared his throat and tapped the gavel lightly against the rostrum.

"Good morning," the president said, straightening his bifocals. "We'll start with our usual introductions, so that the new people will be aware of the company you own or represent." He pulled the microphone to his wide mouth. "We'll start with the table in the back." He looked at Daniella and Brant's table.

Brant stood. "Parker's Art architect. I have ongoing business with George here. He sold me a piece of lake property. I also have ongoing business with Coleen Jones," Brant grinned at Coleen. "She gave me a haircut last night." He patted his wavy hair. "We're also working on the Gains Home Development," Brant said on a more serious note, gesturing to a man sitting at a table at the front of the room. He turned to Daniella. "To my right is Daniella Taylor and she'll be representing Parker's Art when I'm not around."

Daniella stood, greeted the group, and sat down, wanting to wring Brant's neck for forcing her to represent him and his company.

"I don't think it's fair," Daniella leaned closer to Brant and said in a low voice, while the others at their table stood and spoke.

"What's not fair?" Brant asked.

"It wouldn't hurt you to promote the interior design department," Daniella said.

"I do. Everything Parker's Art does is on the business card," Brant replied as he poured himself another cup of coffee.

"Brant, I really think it would be in our best interest if you hired another person to represent Parker's Art," she said.

"That subject is not open for discussion," Brant remarked firmly and took a sip of the coffee.

Daniella tapped the rim of her orange-juice glass. *Not open for discussion huh?* Daniella pondered Brant's words. *We'll see about that.* She cut a small slice of melon in half, stuck it in her mouth, and chewed slowly, while she listened to a well-dressed woman in a navy business suit advertise her small culinary arts school. Several wealthy-looking women sat at a table with the owner of the gourmet cooking school. Their rich gold bracelets and the necklaces encircling their wrists and necks were an indication of their wealth.

Daniella stopped looking at the women and turned her attention back to the meeting. The last member had stood and introduced himself and his company. Daniella barely heard him—her interests were elsewhere, like wondering if the women needed a decorator for their homes. However, she was sure the women's homes were as perfect as their beautiful hairstyles and flawless makeup. Daniella puckered her lips in irritation and glanced at the man who was responsible for snuffing out her creativity.

Wringing Brant's neck would do her about as much good as quitting her job at Parker's Art, she decided, before drinking the last of her orange juice. Inviting Brant over for dinner and becoming his friend made more sense to her. It was a risk she'd have to take, considering the fact that she hadn't had dinner with an attractive man socially for more than two years. Daniella inclined her head and closed her eyes. She was almost ashamed that she would stoop to the level of trickery just to get her decorating job back.

The Business Council's president interrupted Daniella's thoughts. "If there are no more announcements, this meeting is adjourned."

The woman from the culinary arts school rose from her chair and walked over to Daniella.

"I'm Carol Frank," she said, extending her hand. "It's good to have you with us."

"Thank you," Daniella said, standing and shaking Carol's hand, as if she were proud that she was a part of the Business Council's association.

"I own the culinary arts school." Carol said, handing Daniella a business card.

Daniella took the card from the woman and read the gold-etched engravings. The school was not the run-of-the-mill cooking school, but specialized in teaching gourmet and party preparations.

"Is this a two-year cooking course?" Daniella asked, while she looked at the card.

"It is. However, there are many young people having problems preparing food for a simple dinner party, so we decided to add a mini course."

Hmmm, Daniella thought. Gourmet cooking might be what she needed to bring Brant Parker around to her kind of thinking.

"When does the next mini course start?" Daniella asked.

"In two weeks," Carol Frank said.

"Okay, I'll stop by before the end of the week and register," Daniella said. Watching Brant eat had given her the idea to attend the school. On top of that, it would be kind of nice to learn how to cook delicious foods.

"Don't wait long to register Daniella," Carol warned her. "Our vacancy rate is almost nonexistent."

"I'll be there," Daniella said.

"I'll look forward to seeing you." Carol smiled elegantly and moved to another section of the room.

Daniella stuck the business card inside her purse and looked around the room for Brant. She saw him talking to George and another man.

Daniella turned to Monique and Coleen. "It was nice meeting everyone," she said, closing her purse.

"Same here, and we'll be expecting you next week," Coleen said.

Monique nodded in agreement.

Daniella went over to Brant. "I'll see you later."

"All right," Brant said, pushing his hands into his pants' pockets. His lips curved into a satisfied smile as if all was right in his world.

Beverly was opening a box of wallpaper swatches when Daniella walked into the interior design workroom.

"I'm back," Daniella announced as she entered the room, dropping down on the sofa.

"How did the meeting go?" Beverly asked, pushing the swatches aside. She walked over to the sofa and sat next to Daniella.

"It was all right," Daniella said, stretching her legs out before her.

"Yeah?" Beverly smile. "So, I guess you got the chance to flirt with Brant."

It came as no surprise to Daniella that Beverly was

still insisting that she tantalize Brant with her womanly affections. "No, I didn't flirt with Brant. I have no intentions of making him think that I'm interested in anything other than being his friend," Daniella replied keenly.

"Goodness, you don't have to get hostile," Beverly said.

"However, I do have a plan." Daniella winked at Beverly.

"That's my girl," Beverly said. "What is it?"

"No, Beverly, it might not work."

"Ah, you can tell me," Beverly said.

Daniella gave Beverly a half-masked gaze. "You have a habit of discussing everything with that husband of yours. Knowing Tyrone, he'll tell Brant," Daniella reminded Beverly.

"You're right. My husband and I have no secrets. However, I'm willing to keep this information to myself," Beverly declared.

Daniella made a face. Usually, she could trust Beverly. They had been friends for years. They'd attended the same charm school when she was thirteen and Beverly fourteen, they'd also gone to the same church. They had even attended the same college together. Once Daniella and Beverly had thought it was a good idea to have a double wedding. But Daniella had been the first to get married, and Beverly was her maid of honor.

After Daniella and Ray were married, she moved to Florida to live with him. But not many weekends passed that Daniella and Beverly didn't call each other. When Daniella's marriage was in trouble she'd called Beverly and talked and cried. Beverly had listened, giving no advice. Finally, Daniella divorced Ray and moved back to Forest.

Daniella looked at Beverly.

"You know I love you like you were my own flesh-and-blood sister," Daniella said slowly.

"But?" Beverly inquired.

"I think I need to keep this one to myself," Daniella chuckled.

Beverly laughed. "I've got an inkling that Brant is not in for a smooth ride."

"I promise you, he won't know what hit him, until it's done," Daniella said, crossing her fingers.

"All right, Dannie, don't write any checks you can't cash."

"Bev, you worry about me too much," Daniella said. "I have the plan worked out."

Beverly frowned. "I do worry about you. I've seen you get into enough jams over the years," she said, getting up and heading out of the room.

Daniella propped her elbow on the arm of the sofa and rested her chin on her palm, her memory flowed back to the day she met Beverly in New York at Ophelia De 'Vores's school of charm. Daniella had been adamantly against attending the school. She had no desire to walk like a lady. She preferred pitching a baseball for the Dusty Devils and climbing the ladder to Jerry's tree house, with him and his sister. Jerry had been Daniella and his sister's "tomboy" trainer, showing the girls how to throw uppercuts and left-right punches, so they could protect themselves if ever they needed to when he wasn't around to defend them.

Daniella dismissed her childhood deliberations when

Beverly came back carrying two cans of cola. She gave one to Daniella and popped the tab on hers.

"After the work I did this morning, and worrying about how you and Brant were getting along, I need some caffeine." Beverly took a sip from the soda.

"You can stop worrying because I have everything under control. And it doesn't include seducing Brant," Daniella replied.

"Speaking of worrying," Beverly said, "I, or you, received a call from that nut this morning."

A flicker of fear swept through Daniella. She needed to put an end to this phone harassment.

"What did he say this time?" Daniella asked.

"He asked for his money. I reminded him that he'd given the antiques to us."

"Beverly you told him right. I'm not paying him one red cent," Daniella said.

"He didn't know what I was talking about," Beverly said.

"So, we're dealing with a real nutcase here?" Daniella inquired.

"Uh huh, once he realized that he wasn't speaking to you, he said that you had his money and he wanted every dollar of it back," Beverly said.

"Money, what money?" Daniella rose from the couch.

Beverly shrugged. "I don't know."

Befuddled, Daniella racked her brain trying to figure out who she owed other than the mortgage company—and of course she had a balance on her credit cards. But those companies were professional, they didn't call their clients and breathe on the phone and leave threatening messages even if she had been late paying them.

Daniella ran her fingers through her hair. "Did you star six-nine the number?"

"Yes, and the operator couldn't give me the number, I called the trace operator." Beverly sighed. "The number came from a pay phone," Beverly said.

"I don't understand this." Daniella went to the phone. "I refuse to have a nut harassing me." She dialed Jerry's number. He was a private detective now. Jerry was like a hunting dog, he didn't stop until he had found what he was looking for. She turned to Beverly while waiting for Jerry's office to answer her call. "Lord, I have enough problems in my life without having a crazy man calling me," Daniella stated, tapping the tips of her nails against the countertop.

"I heard that," Beverly said.

"Hello, is Jerry in?" Daniella said to Jerry's secretary. She listened for a moment. "Tell him to give Daniella Taylor a call as soon as he returns. Thank you." Daniella hung up and planted both hands on her hips. "If I didn't need Jerry, he would be all in the way. Now that I want to see him, I can't find him."

CHAPTER 4

Brant sat on the bench in the locker room, resting his back against the cement wall, cooling down from his evening workout. He allowed his mind to wander to his hectic schedule. He barely had time for himself anymore. He worked all of fifteen hours a day. As a result, his social life had gone to hell in a handbasket. It wasn't as if he couldn't have a passionate relationship with a woman. Glenda was a willing candidate. Thinking of her brought to mind the gold neck chain she had bought for him. The way his work schedule was going, he would never have time to take the gift back to Glenda. Brant rubbed his hand over his face.

It was a pity that he hadn't thought of his social life until he and Daniella began working closely. Sometimes in the middle of the night, Brant woke up, thinking about Daniella. He could almost smell the soft scent of her perfume, the way her lips curved into a smile whenever she was happy—and when she was frustrated, especially with him, how her full lips pouted.

But somehow, thinking of Daniella was a waste of time. She was probably still pining over her ex-husband. On top of that, Daniella had practically ignored him since she had been rehired at Parker's Art. Their conversations were limited to the subject of their work. Other than that, Daniella hardly spoke. Brant thought of Daniella as he stood and crossed the floor to his locker and took out his faded blue jeans and gray sleeveless T-shirt.

Daniella had once been fun, Brant thought, remembering the evening after the company's picnic how he had kissed her. He had wanted Daniella then, but he had wanted to own Parker's Art more. Some brownnoser had informed his father that he and Daniella were acting like lovers instead of employees the day of the picnic. Brant had felt like a young boy when his father confronted him with the information.

In some ways, he had been a boy. He hadn't stood up to his father and fought for the right to love Daniella. Brant stepped into his jeans, and then put on his shirt. He had regretted that he had chosen his work over Daniella, but at the time, it had made sense. All of his life, he had wanted to own Parker's Art. He owned the company now and the woman that he carried a secret torch for didn't know he was alive.

Brant slammed the locker door. The sound of the metal thwacking against the steel sent James Amour running from one of the shower stalls in the back, spilling generic ammonia on his way to the front of the locker room. The strong aroma of the disinfectant scented the air. Brant picked up his duffel bag, and headed out of the room.

"What's up?" James stopped Brant.

Brant wheeled around, tilting his head to the side. He'd never paid much attention to the janitor. James's tannish-brown oily complexion shone like new copper. His hawk eyes looked out from underneath thick, bushy black brows.

"Yeah?" Brant said, lifting his gaze to meet the janitor's.

James screwed the cap on the ammonia, then gave Brant a wry grin.

"I—ah—well, I'm looking for extra work," James said. "I thought maybe I could get a job with your company. I—ah—I saw an ad in the paper."

James obviously thought Parker's Art needed a janitor, Brant decided after listening to the man stammer. James was an excellent cleaning man. He maintained the gym, keeping the place sparkling. However, Parker's Art needed a licensed carpenter.

"I don't need a janitor," Brant said, turning to leave.

"Wait a minute. I don't have a carpenter's license or anything, but I'm a good handyman," James said. There was a faint trace of sadness in his eyes. "I've got the experience as a laborer on construction sites too," James said, explaining to Brant how he had worked part-time as a construction laborer and handyman while he was in school.

Parker's Art had recently hired laborers for the construction part of the company, Brant recalled watching James. So far, he didn't need another employee. But, Brant thought, James would be perfect for fixing up the lake house he'd bought a few months ago. Brant glanced at the man standing before him. If any other man would've come to him pleading for a job he didn't have, he would have flatly refused him. For some reason, James Amour was an interesting man. Regardless of the fact that James's mendicant appearance resembled a beachcomber, Brant mused as he carefully evaluated the janitor, he seemed intelligent. Everybody fell on hard times every once in a while. If he could help a brother out, why not? Brant thought, not overlooking the fact that he loved to help people.

"All right, I have a house on the lake that needs a lot of repairs. If you can fix doors, patch walls, and paint, the job is yours," Brant said.

"All right!" James said, grinning. "When do I start?"

"Stop by Parker's Art in the morning and fill out an application."

"One other thing," James said, before Brant left the locker room. "If it's okay with you, can I live in the house while I fix it?"

Brant thought about James's question for a second or two.

"Yeah." Brant shrugged.

"Thanks, Mr. Parker," James said.

Brant nodded. "Just call me Brant. And you're welcome," Brant replied, checking his watch. It was going on eleven o'clock. He wondered if Daniella was awake. His uncle had some old houses in Georgia that he wanted Parker's Art to renovate. He'd called Brant earlier that day, asking if he could come down and get the job started.

Brant planned to start work on his uncle's houses in a few weeks. He had been busy and had forgotten to tell Daniella about their trip to Georgia.

Brant weaved his way through the rows of exercise bikes. The whining sound of treadmills distracted Brant's thoughts. Ducking his head, Brant moved through the door leading to the lobby, and headed out to his truck. It seemed too late to call Daniella, Brant thought, climbing into his pickup. But he wanted to prepare her for the trip. He took his cellular phone from his gym bag and called her. When he didn't get an answer, Brant decided to drive out to her house.

Pink and brown Tudor-roof town homes stood across the street from the park, like pretty dollhouses. Brant pressed the brakes and drove around the bend. He noticed that Daniella's porch light was on when he pulled into her driveway. He got out, and rang her doorbell. Seconds passed before Daniella opened the door. When she finally opened it, Brant's gaze shifted from the surprised expression in her eyes to her cherry-red lips. He lowered his lids and cast a lingering glance on the black silk knee-length lounge outfit she was wearing. Brant raised his glance just enough to gaze a moment at Daniella's cashmere cleavage. He swallowed.

"Can I come in?" Brant asked, glancing at her.

"Sure. Is everything all right?" Daniella moved aside.

"Yeah." Brant glanced around Daniella's living room, at the pastel-blue sofa, the color of a clear summer's sky sitting against the wall. White, crimson, and straw-yellow pillows the shape of flower petals nestled against the sofa's plump cushions. "You left today before I could tell you about the project we'll be working on in Georgia," Brant said.

"You could've call me," Daniella said, looking at Brant.

"I did, but you didn't answer the phone. Anyway, I have to be in New York tomorrow and I thought I'd better tell you," Brant said.

"Okay," Daniella said, closing the door. "Would you like something to drink?" she asked turning toward the kitchen.

"I'll take a bottle of seltzer if you have it," Brant said, moving farther inside.

"Sit down." Daniella gestured to the sofa and started toward to the kitchen.

"I'm sorry if I stopped you from reading," Brant said, checking out the romance novel that was laying facedown next to him.

"It's all right," Daniella called from the kitchen.

Brant leaned back against the sofa's cushions and glanced around Daniella's living room.

Two gas oak logs sat inside Daniella's fake fireplace. A couple of green ivy plants sat in silver pots on each side of the mantle. The room was stamped with Daniella's profession. He understood why she was upset at losing the job she loved. *But I need her more,* Brant thought, watching Daniella as she walked in the room carrying a wooden serving tray with a plate filled with finger sandwiches and a small crystal bowl filled with cashew nuts, water, and two mini bottles of beer.

Brant took the bottle of seltzer and two mugs off

the tray as soon as she set the tray on the glass table. He removed the cap from the bottle and glanced at the two bottles of beer on the tray.

"I felt like drinking a beer," Daniella said, taking the bottle of beer from the tray and filling a frosty mug with the sudsy brew. "I brought one for you, just in case you changed your mind." Daniella smiled at him.

Brant grinned. It never occurred to him that she drank the stuff. Most women he knew pretended they drank only wine.

"I think I'll pass," he said, still grinning, while Daniella took a cashew nut from the bowl. "But I'll have one of these," Brant said, taking a finger sandwich, popping it into his mouth,

Brant turned the seltzer water up to his mouth, drinking half the contents before setting the bottle on the coaster. He shifted his gaze to Daniella's face, observing her sensual red lips.

"So. . .what're we doing in Georgia?" Daniella asked, folding her legs underneath her.

"Believe me, Dannie, it's not going to be exciting," Brant said, telling Daniella about the job his uncle had hired Parker's Art to do. All the while he was talking to her, he noticed how attractive she was. A thick, black, shiny mass of curls hung past her shoulders.

"It can't be that bad. I love going to Atlanta," Daniella replied.

For a moment Brant gazed at Daniella. She looked sweet and loving sitting on her legs, nibbling cashew nuts, and sipping beer. Brant wished he could hold her. But instead, he interrupted Daniella's fantasy about them going to Atlanta.

"We're not going to Atlanta, Dannie," Brant said, putting another sandwich in his mouth and washing it down with seltzer.

"Exactly where are we going, Brant?" Daniella asked, looking at him.

Brant set the bottle down and cast a quick glance at his assistant. It was clear that he had some major explaining to do regarding their trip to Georgia.

"We're going to east Georgia, Dannie," he said, hoping that they wouldn't have another heated discussion. Tonight, he felt like being at peace with her.

"In other words, we're going to the backwoods," Daniella implicated.

Brant pushed to the edge of the sofa and turned to Daniella. Her jet-black eyes were masked with disappointment.

"Let's just say we're going to a small town," Brant said.

"Do I have to go Brant. . .because I really don't want to."

Brant Parker leaned back against the sofa to get a better look at the woman who was calmly refusing to take the trip with him. Could he force her to take the trip? He most certainly could.

"It's not a matter of you wanting to go," Brant said, "I'm telling you that you're going."

Daniella dropped the half-eaten finger sandwich on the tray, and turned to face Brant.

"Visiting a site in the backwoods of Georgia is not a good idea for me, Brant. I understand my position, but this is short notice and I promised Beverly that

I would work a few nights with her to finish a project,"
Daniella stated.

"Beverly can find someone else to help her," Brant
remarked.

Daniella placed her hands in her lap and began
tapping her fingers against the silk lounger. "Why
can't Tyrone go with you?" she asked.

Brant leaned forward. How was he going to deal
with a woman as lovely and stubborn as Daniella? He
had fought with her once, and he would do it again.
He gazed at her soft, manicured hands resting on
her silk-covered lap. Tonight, he didn't want to have
a heated confrontation with Daniella. He was tired.

"I didn't come over here to fight with you, Dannie,"
Brant finally said. "Are you going to work with me
willingly or do I have to find someone else to get the
job done?" he asked, noticing her cool gaze.

"Okay, Brant." Daniella uncoiled her legs and slid
off the sofa. She crossed the floor and opened the
door. "I'll go to Georgia. After all, it is my new job,"
she lamented.

By the time Brant reached the door, Daniella's
expression hadn't warmed.

"We'll discuss the trip in more detail," Brant said,
walking out on the porch, shifting his gaze to her red
lips.

"Good night Brant," Daniella said.

Brant lowered his head and walked out to his
pickup. The loud slam of Daniella's front door was
a sure indication that she was upset with him for
dragging her to the backwoods of Georgia. And having Daniella upset with him was the last thing he
wanted. It wasn't good for their working relationship

and it definitely wasn't good for any intimate plans he had for them.

Brant sat in his truck gazing at Daniella's house for a few minutes before he started the pickup's engine. He wondered what Daniella would do if he asked her to be his lover. One of these days, he was going to find out. But in the meantime he planned to proceed with caution.

CHAPTER 5

"If it's not the man who gave us the antique furniture, then who's making the obscene phone calls, Jerry?" Daniella was worried. It had taken Jerry three days to get back to her and now he was confirming what she already suspected. Someone was stalking her. What Daniella couldn't figure out was why.

"After I made a few phone calls around New Jersey, I followed my hunch and called Florida." Jerry Mack gave Daniella a side glance. He was thirty-eight years old, with skin the color of creamed chocolate, and was exactly six feet tall. He could've played professional basketball. Jerry chose a profession that he had a passion for: private investigating.

"Why would you do a thing like that?" Daniella asked.

"Your ex-husband dealt with a lot of shady characters, Dannie," Jerry reminded her.

"Don't remind me," Daniella said, glancing around the park. The pink and purple hues lacing the early evening sky were like a background for the pitch pines and red oaks that seemed to capture the sadness that welled up inside her.

"Did you know that Ray went to jail for embezzling money from the accounting firm he worked for?" Jerry asked Daniella.

"No. When did that happened?" Daniella asked, not a bit surprised that Ray had gotten arrested for stealing money.

"He went to prison about six months after you divorced him." Jerry said. He walked over to Daniella. "I don't know how to say this to you, but. . ."

"Just say it, Jerry," Daniella said. She hated when people spared her feelings.

"Dannie, he got out of prison and he died," Jerry added, cooling Daniella's curiosity.

"Okay," Daniella said slowly. Ray Spencer was the most disgusting person she'd ever known. If she would've known that he was the world's biggest jerk, she would've never married him. As it turned out, Ray was a genius at concealing his real image. After they were married, Ray showed his true colors.

"Are you all right?" Jerry asked.

"I'm fine," Daniella said, thinking of Ray's Aunt Minnie. Minnie had a fit when she learned that Daniella was divorcing her nephew. She believed that women were to stand by their husbands no matter what problems they had. Daniella raked her fingers through her hair. It was too bad that Minnie hadn't thought it was Ray who ruined the marriage, Daniella decided.

"Just checking," Jerry replied.

"How did Ray die?" Daniella asked.

"Ray and some friends got caught in a storm while fishing. The boat sank." Jerry glanced at Daniella as if to see her reaction to the news of her ex-husband's death.

"Jerry, first of all, I can't afford to pay off Ray's old debts," Daniella said, concluding that the phone calls could be some of Ray's hooligan friends. Did you find out how much money Ray owed this person."

"I'm not sure, Dannie," Jerry said. "But I intend to find out. It's important that you know what you're up against," Jerry replied.

Black fear floated over Daniella. She placed her hands on her hips and started moving toward her house across the street.

"Jerry, please find this person and have him put behind bars."

"I'm working on a case in Florida. While I'm there, I'll check things out," Jerry assured Daniella.

Daniella gave Jerry a wry smile. "If I were paying you, you would treat this like it was a real case . . . right?"

"That's not true and you know it," Jerry said, as they walked out of the park.

The fear that coiled in Daniella seemed to have tied tiny knots in her stomach.

Jerry unlocked his car door. "Dannie, don't worry, I'll call you and set up a meeting as soon as I get back in town."

"Thanks Jerry," Daniella said, checking her watch. In thirty minutes, her gourmet cooking class began. She ran across the street to her house and took her purse from the bedroom closet, dismissing the disturbing news that Jerry had told her about Ray.

Daniella slid behind the steering wheel and started the Jeep's engine and switched on the headlights. As she backed the Jeep out of the driveway, a disquieting thought flitted across her mind. She had noticed how relaxed and comfortable Brant was the night he had stopped by her place. When she found herself reacting to his charisma, she had just about thrown him out. It wasn't because she was angry at him because of his decision to take her to the backwoods of Georgia to work for his uncle. It was the way her heart fluttered when her gaze had met his.

I think it would be a wise idea to invite Beverly and Tyrone over for dinner, too, Daniella mused. Being alone with Brant could lead to complications. After they discussed their work, she was sure that Brant would keep his promise and start asking her questions about her personal life. Having the Coles over would put an end to that conversation, Daniella decided, turning on the radio.

A love song from the sixties floated out of the Jeep's speakers, reminding Daniella of how carefree she had been before she had met and married Ray.

Daniella pulled up in the school's parking lot and parked between a Jaguar and a Mercedes. She got out and walked across the lot to the culinary arts school.

A middle-aged woman with a short bob hairstyle was perched on a stool behind the registration desk. Her rose-colored lips curved into a smile when Daniella walked up to the counter, spoke, and handed the clerk her computerized card. While Daniella waited for the clerk to sign her in, she looked over the clerk's shoulder at the shelves of cookbooks. Pictures of beef, lamb, and chicken dinners with long-stem goblets filled with red or white wine sat next to the food. Daniella smiled to herself. The glossy food photos had a subliminal way of making her hungry.

The clerk lifted the glasses that hung around her neck on a silver chain to her eyes, and slid the white plastic card through the computer's slot.

"The class is being held in the second room down the hall to your left," she said to Daniella, pointing a long rose-polished fingernail toward the doorway.

"Thanks," Daniella said. She had almost forgotten that tonight the class was making a dinner for one of their examinations.

On the far side of the room were stoves, refrigerators, and cabinets. An easel stood in the center of the floor in front of a long conference table. The menu for the night was written on the board.

Daniella walked over to a table, sat next to Coleen, and read the menu on the chalkboard. Stuffed chicken with apple glaze, steamed broccoli with cauliflower and red peppers, and *acini di pepe* fruit pudding.

"I hope that Carol doesn't expect me to make a perfect sauce tonight," Daniella said to Coleen, rolling her eyes to the ceiling.

"Don't worry about it," Coleen said, "she'll give you the recipes and you can practice at home."

"Thank God." Daniella chuckled, deciding that she would serve this meal to Brant. She looked at Coleen. "How do you know she'll give us the recipes?"

Coleen smiled. "Girl, I flunked the first class. I burned the chicken and the bread."

Daniella laughed just as Carol Frank walked in and stood before the class.

Carol was a short woman about five feet tall with wide hips and a pretty smile.

"Is everyone ready to cook their first gourmet meal?"

Carol smiled, showing her beautiful white teeth.

An assortment of mumbles and shuffling papers could be heard throughout the room from the students.

"I'm not sure about the sauce for the chicken," Daniella said, worried that she would overcook the mixture.

"You won't have a problem as long as you follow the recipe," Carol said, glancing to the end of the table, recognizing Monique, who was holding up her hand.

"Yes?" Miss Frank said.

"I personally think that we should use frozen vegetables, because when I get home from work, I'm too tired to look at fresh vegetables, let alone clean and cut them," Monique said.

Carol Frank took a few steps toward her students.

"I think more than half of the women who work will agree with you. But in this class, we use only fresh ingredients."

Daniella twisted in her chair, silently agreeing with Monique. She doubted that Brant would let her leave work early just to prepare fresh vegetables.

By the end of the class, Daniella set her dishes on the table. The smell of baked chicken with apple glaze filled the room. Daniella took a knife and sliced a tiny piece of the chicken. She tasted the tender meat, closing her eyes, savoring the delicious flavor. "Ummm hmmm." Daniella smiled, satisfied with her new culinary skills. The dinner was tasty enough to turn an enemy into a friend.

After class, Daniella packed her dinner in a basket that she'd borrowed from Miss Frank and drove home. If she couldn't win Brant over with her cooking, she had another ace up her sleeve. She wasn't a betting woman, but she would play Brant at a game of pool to get her job back. If she lost . . . it was a risk she had to take, and riding on the wing of that bright idea came the question: Would Brant be willing to bet her for the job she wanted?

Ten minutes later, Daniella pulled up into her driveway and cut off the motor. Just as she turned off the Jeep's headlights, her next-door neighbor, Grace Mills walked outside and stood on her porch. The elderly woman lifted her Pomeranian in her wrinkled arms and gently stroked the animal's tan fur with her orange fingernails.

"That man was over here. He left about ten minutes ago," Grace Mills said, glancing at Daniella from underneath her long false lashes.

Daniella slammed her Jeep's door, and walked to her porch.

"What man?" Daniella asked, afraid that Ray's horrible friend had paid her a visit.

"The man who drives the white pickup," Mrs. Mills said.

"Oh," Daniella replied nonchalantly and went to her Jeep 4x4 for the food. The fear that swept through her subsided as she wondered what Brant wanted.

"Is he your friend?" Grace asked.

Daniella drew in a long breath and let it out slowly. Her parents had raised her to respect her elders, nosy or otherwise. But Mrs. Mills was the nosiest woman she'd ever known.

"That man that was here tonight is my boss," Daniella stated.

"Ummm hmmm," Grace said. "He looks like a fine young fellow." Grace stroked the animal's head.

Daniella's face warmed with frustration. "Good night, Mrs. Mills." Daniella unlocked her front door and went inside. She picked up the note that Brant had slipped through her mail slot.

Dannie, call me at home.
Brant

A touch of impetuousness caressed Daniella's heart. *What's so important that Brant has to talk to me tonight,* she thought, going to the kitchen to put away the dinner. She set the last container in the freezer and went upstairs to her bathroom. She needed to take a shower to wash off the scent of baked chicken and *acini di pepe* fruit pudding.

Minutes later, Daniella's shower was finished. She went to her bedroom closet and slipped a lavender silk gown from the rack. She stuck her feet into a pair of white bedroom slippers and went to call Brant.

Daniella sat on the bed next to the nightstand and dialed Brant's number. On the fourth ring, Brant answered the phone.

"Hello," Brant's voice came across the line, sending unwanted shivers through her.

"I got your note," she said, resting her back against the headboard.

"Where were you?" Brant inquired.

The low, concerned sound in Brant's voice sent another quiver through her. Daniella smiled wryly. If she hadn't been aware of his and Glenda's relationship, she could've easily read more into what he was saying.

"I was out. What's so important that I have to call you in the middle of the night?" she asked, kicking off her bedroom slippers and scooting under the sheets.

Brant was silent. If it wasn't for his soft breathing, Daniella might have thought he had hung up.

"I'm going to North Carolina tomorrow, I'll be in Rocky Mountain. I'll be back Saturday morning."

"Do I have to go with you?" Daniella asked.

"No. Can you handle things while I'm gone?"

Irritation because she had been dragged from her natural line of work to argue with contractors and carpenters was enough to make her grit her teeth.

"When did you decide to take this trip?" she asked.

"The project in North Carolina is finished and I need to make sure the building meets all requirements," Brant said.

"Hmmm," Daniella murmured.

"Do you have a problem with that?" Brant asked.

"No, I'm planning a small dinner party and I wanted to invite you," she replied.

Brant chuckled. "I thought you offered finger sandwiches to people you didn't like."

"Where did you get that wild idea from?" Daniella questioned his concept concerning her attitude toward him.

"For some reason I get the feeling that I'm not your favorite person," Brant said.

"I like you. I would like your friendship," Daniella said.

"What kind of friendship?" Brant asked.

"A platonic friendship would be nice," Daniella replied.

"Platonic, huh?" Brant implored.

"I don't see any reason why we can't have a friendly boss-employee relationship," Daniella said. At this point she didn't care what Brant thought of her.

"First of all, Dannie, I have to be honest with you. I can't be just your friend," Brant said.

Imaginary butterflies fluttered Daniella's stomach. *Lord, if Brant doesn't want my friendship, I'm dead in the water,* she thought.

"And why not?" Daniella composed herself.

"I'll leave that alone because I've got a feeling that you're still hung up on your ex-husband." Brant chuckled.

"What?" Daniella rose up in bed. Brant's soft chuckle pulsated against her eardrums, making her heart do a flip-flop.

"We'll discuss it more at your dinner party," Brant said, still chuckling under his breath.

"Good night, Brant." Daniella placed the receiver on its cradle and pulled the white sheet up around her shoulders.

Suddenly, she was no longer sleepy. The terrifying thought of Brant's intimate interest in her made her uncomfortable. She was aware of her frozen passion, which thawed each time she was near him. But tonight, she had learned exactly how Brant felt about her. As long as he didn't make any designing moves on her emotions, she would be fine.

Daniella snuggled further under the covers. Suddenly a disconcerting thought crept across her mind. Brant thought she loved Ray? She banished the thought, drifting off into her own private world of dreams.

Brant's breath was hot, fanning against the hollow of her neck. Slowly, he raised his head and kissed her rising chest, allowing his lips to stroke her breasts lightly until they peaked from desire, need, and plain old-fashioned passion. Without warning, Brant's lips touched hers, kissing her until she was out of control. Soft moans slipped from her throat as his warm hand slipped the silk gown up over her hips.

With sizzling passion, Daniella pulled Brant's muscular body closer to hers, stroking his chest and back, feeling his strong thighs against hers.

Six o'clock. The alarm clock jolted Daniella out of her slumber.

"Oh my God!" Daniella sat up in bed, gazing at her surroundings. She glanced over at the empty side of the bed. *Lord don't let me lose my mind,* she prayed, thankful that Brant would be out of town for a few days. After that dream, she wasn't so sure she could look at him with a straight face.

Daniella laid in bed for a moment before getting up to take her shower. *Girl, get a grip,* she thought, trying to delete the passionate dreams she'd had of Brant Parker from her mind. She had other things to think about besides some silly dream, she decided, making a mental note of the things she had to do before the day was over. She got out of bed and headed for the shower.

First of all, she had to go shopping for a dress for the Women's Charity Ball and she definitely wanted to have lunch with Beverly, and catch up on all the latest gossip.

Daniella stepped out of the shower, wrapped herself in a plush white towel, and went to her closet. She took out a yellow flare-tailed sundress and a pair of barebacked heels. She had only a couple of hours of work in the office, as long as there were no problems. On her lunch break she planned to take care of personal errands.

Daniella got dressed and drove to the office. A couple of security guards and the receptionist were the only employees in the building. Daniella greeted them cheerfully and went to her and Brant's work area. As usual, the room was neat, cool, and smelled of country flower air freshener.

Architect plan #408 sat in the file on Daniella's workstation. She opened the file and checked the plan, making sure she'd made all corrections to the new development Brant had assigned her to work on. Suddenly, without warning, Daniella thought of her dinner invitation to Brant. She couldn't remember the last time she'd had a social dinner with a man. It's business, she thought. A mocking voice in the back of her mind warned her differently. Daniella wondered if her intentions were subconsciously driven toward becoming Brant's friend or if she wanted him for a lover. Please, Daniella thought, as a shiver danced up her spine. She could never trust herself to love another man.

However, Brant was everything she'd dreamed of in a man. He was chivalrous, charismatic, and drop-dead handsome. While Daniella sorted and weighed her options for a man that had the power to make her legs go weak and her heart do flip-flops, she could no longer deny the shocking truth: She was attracted to Brant, which meant she must be careful.

Daniella completed the plan she'd been working on

and took her purse and walked down to the interior design department to invite Beverly to have lunch with her.

"Are you having lunch with Tyrone?" Daniella stuck her head inside the door and asked Beverly.

"I don't think so," Beverly said, looking up from her work. "You're looking cute today." She smiled. "What's the occasion?"

I'm going to the mall to buy my dress for the charity ball," Daniella said, glancing around at the work area she loved.

"You know, I almost forgot about that Women's Charity Ball," Beverly said, pushing the stencil that she was working on aside, and going to get her purse from the closet.

"Well, let's go before the stores and restaurant get too crowded," Daniella said. "Oh, I'm having a dinner party and you, Tyrone, and Brant are invited."

"That sounds nice." Beverly smiled at her girl-friend. "Of course we'll be there."

"Good," Daniella said. Her worries about things getting serious between her and Brant were over.

"Is Brant taking you to the charity ball?" Beverly asked as they walked out of the building to Daniella's Jeep.

"What makes you think that he's my date?" Daniella asked.

"You're inviting him to dinner. I thought maybe . . ." Beverly started.

"You know my reasons for inviting Brant to dinner," Daniella interrupted Beverly.

Beverly slid onto the passenger's seat, casting a glance at Daniella. "I also know you." She gave Daniella an impish grin.

"If you're suggesting that I like Brant more than I should . . . I do, but Beverly, you know my problem and right now I'm not sure if I can handle an intimate relationship."

Daniella turned the key in the ignition and started the motor.

Beverly laughed. "It's not like you don't know him, Dannie." Beverly smiled. "You guys will make a perfect couple."

"I don't know about that," Daniella said.

"Dannie, Brant is not stupid, if he finds out that you're using him, you're going to regret this scheme," Beverly reminded her. "Besides, I think he's got the hots for you."

"I'm not sure about that either. But just in case, you and Tyrone are invited to dinner too. That way things won't have a chance to get out of hand," Daniella said, pulling out onto Edison Avenue into the noon traffic headed to the mall. Beverly was right, Brant wasn't a man she could play with. Daniella's plans were for her and Brant's relationship to remain employer and employee. If they were lucky enough to become casual friends, she would be grateful, which meant any flames he had sparked around her heart would dissolve.

"Look, I promised to take things slow after I divorced Ray. I'm sure I'll meet a nice man one day," Daniella said, turning onto the street that took them to the mall.

"I think that you've met him," Beverly said.

Daniella stopped at the traffic light, ignoring her girlfriend. She didn't have time to clutter her life with a man.

"How's the baby?" she asked, changing the subject,

then realized that was not the right question to ask. It always gave Beverly the opportunity to start harping on her about remarrying and starting a family. Beverly of all people knew how much she wanted at least one child.

Beverly cut her eye at Daniella and smothered a smile. "T.J. is fine," she said. "Did you get the invitation to his birthday party?"

"Not yet," Daniella said, and held her breath for a second, expecting Beverly to remind her of her ticking biological clock.

Daniella found a parking space close to the entrance of the mall and cut off the Jeep's engine.

"I hope the boutique didn't sell that dress," Daniella said to Beverly as she walked inside the mall, heading toward the evening wear shop.

"I doubt it," Beverly said, as they walked into the boutique and toward the evening gown section.

Daniella bought the black, short, tight dress with the low-cut back and spaghetti straps that she wanted.

Beverly purchased a white party dress. They headed to the shoe store. Daniella bought black heels with a splash of gold across the toe. Their next stop was the jewelry store.

As usual, Daniella browsed at the jewels in the showcases before going inside the store. Gold and silver pieces of expensive jewels sat on red velvet. Expensive engagement and wedding rings rested in black velvet boxes.

Daniella had glanced up from admiring the diamonds and started inside, when she saw Brant and Glenda standing at the counter in the jewelry shop. Glenda hung on to Brant's arm as if it were a life jacket as she whispered in his ear. Suddenly, Glenda turned and gave Daniella an icy glare.

Struggling with a raw, sick feeling that raced through her, Daniella walked away from the jewelry shop window. How could she have been gullible enough to believe a word Brant had said. Daniella glanced around for Beverly. She had been in such a hurry to accessorize her dress that she hadn't noticed that Beverly had gone to another store. Daniella walked around the corner and sat on one of the mall benches. She needed time out. Whatever unsettling thoughts she had about seeing Brant in the jewelry shop with his lover was no business of hers, Daniella decided. After a short while, she pulled herself together and went to find Beverly, who had made her way to the Tote's and Things clothing store.

Daniella walked to the check-out counter where Beverly was purchasing a gift for T.J.

"I'm starving," Daniella said.

"Me, too," Beverly remarked, taking the change the cashier was handing her. She stuck the bills in her purse and walked out with Daniella.

"I want Chinese food for lunch," Daniella said.

"Chinese sounds good to me," Beverly stated.

"Ummm hmmm," Daniella smiled. Her face was cheerful, but her heart sobbed while suspicion gnawed at her. Why hadn't Brant gone to North Carolina? she questioned herself. She quickly dismissed her thoughts, reminding herself that what Brant did with his time was none of her business.

Daniella and Beverly found a table up front near the window in the Chinese restaurant. A waiter took their orders as soon as they sat. Daniella ordered Lobster Cantonese. Beverly ordered Curry Shrimp.

While they waited for their food, Daniella was quiet. Too quiet. Just seeing Brant with Glenda was disturbing enough, but in the jewelry store? Why would Brant tell her he was going to North Carolina if he wanted to take the day off to be with his girlfriend? Men! Daniella thought, recalling her phone conversation with him last night.

"What's wrong with you?" Beverly cut into Daniella's deliberations.

Daniella traced the rim of her water glass before answering Beverly.

"Nothing," she said. Discussing her problems with Beverly wouldn't help her feel better.

Beverly looked at Daniella. "I saw them too."

"So?" Daniella said.

"Looks can be deceiving." Beverly consoled Daniella.

Daniella gave Beverly a half-masked stare. "I'm fine!" She wrinkled her nose playfully, just before the waiter came over and set their order in front of them.

Daniella and Beverly ate their food, not saying much to each other. From time to time, Daniella's thoughts slipped back to Brant. Why would he want her to think that he was interested in having more than a platonic relationship with her? Daniella shrugged. She hoped that Brant wasn't a player. She banished the thoughts and tried to eat the food that she loved. It wasn't working, the food tasted like sawdust.

After work that day, Daniella stopped by her house long enough to change into black leotards, a black

Danskin top, thick white socks, and dance shoes. She packed a duffel bag with a pair of jeans, a T-shirt, and sneakers to change into after her dance class was over.

Volunteering kept her mind free of her ruined marriage and messy divorce and now it served the purpose of shielding her thoughts of Brant. Tonight she would stretch and dance until she was too exhausted to think about Brant.

Just as Daniella climbed into her Jeep, Grace Mills walked out of her town house pulling her Pomeranian on his red leash. "Hi," the elderly, sophisticated woman spoke to Daniella.

Lord, what does Grace Mills want now? Daniella thought before returning the greeting to her neighbor. "Hello, Mrs. Mills." Daniella forced herself to smile.

"You know, Dannie, if you don't have a date to the Women's Charity Ball, my son Charlie will be happy to escort you," Grace offered, as if Charlie needed her to solicit a date for him.

"Your son?" Daniella asked, remembering when she first returned to New Jersey, Grace had invited her and her parents to a dinner party. Grace had neglected to tell Daniella that Charlie was also invited. Charlie was handsome, tall, and the color of mahogany. He had one problem: He bragged about his money, his property, and how the women loved him. That night over dinner, Charlie had managed to pluck Daniella's nerves. She lied to keep from telling Grace that she didn't want to go with her son.

"Oh, so the young man is taking you?" Grace pried.

Daniella swallowed hard. Another lie. "Yes," she said, starting the engine and backing out of her driveway as quickly as she could without driving into an oncoming car. Please! Daniella thought, glancing at Grace, who was still standing in her yard.

Daniella kept her thoughts clear of Brant while she drove to the community center. Thinking too much about Brant Parker wasn't good for her nerves.

Several teenage girls from the swim team sat on the cement steps of the community center, chit-chatting and giggling when Daniella walked past them on her way to the dance studio.

On her way down the hall, Daniella passed the gym. The scent of ammonia mingled with sweat, and cologne floated through the open door. She glanced inside the room. At first she thought that the basket-ball coach was Brant. He had the same black, wavy hair and his stance resembled Brant's. The basketball coach turned and faced the entrance. Daniella real-ized her mistake. She should've known Brant didn't have time to volunteer his services, or did he? Was he too busy lying about where he spent his time. *Like I care,* Daniella mused, glancing at the long-legged boys in oversized gym shorts scrambling across the floor, hustling for the basketball. The sound of their rubber soles squeaking against the varnished floors produced goose bumps on her skin.

Daniella arranged her duffel bag comfortably on her shoulder and moved down the hall to her class-room.

Ten girls dressed in tights and leotards were stretch-ing on the bar in front of the mirrored walls when Daniella walked into the studio.

"Hey you guys!" Daniella greeted the girls.

"What's up, Miss Taylor," the girls said in unison.

"Are you ready to rock and roll?" Daniella slipped a disc into the stereo.

"Yeah," the girls answered.

"Then let's get busy," Daniella said, chuckling. She led the girls into a warm-up stretch and soon ten pairs of steel tap shoes clicked against the floor like a thousand tiny hammers.

As the taps clicked to the beat of the music, thoughts of Brant ran through Daniella's mind. Why had he lied to her? She had thought Brant was a man with integrity. But lately, as always, she had made a mistake in judging men.

Daniella directed the tap dance to a slower pace, and finally she directed the dancers to stop.

"Take a break," she said, going over to change the music in the stereo. We're practicing our run, jump, flip in the next session," she said.

"Can we take fifteen minutes?" one of the girls asked.

"I don't think so." Daniella looked to see which girl wanted more than the regular ten-minute break.

"Ah, come on, Miss Taylor. The juice machine is broken and I need to go to the store."

Daniella gave the girl a brief, stern look. "Okay, but hurry back."

"Thanks, Miss Taylor," the girl said, running out of the studio.

Daniella shook her head, remembering the day that her mother had made her take dance lessons. She'd loved them with a passion.

Daniella slipped the disc into the player and reached for the headphones to check the music. Just as she picked up the headphones, someone tapped on the door. Thinking that the girls were back to ask for five more minutes, Daniella turned around.

Glenda stood facing her. Her auburn neck-length hair was wet and limp from her aerobics class.

"I need to talk to you," Glenda said to Daniella.

"About what?" Daniella dropped the headphones on top of the stereo.

"You need to understand a few things about me and Brant." Glenda walked farther into the studio.

"Why?" Daniella asked, not missing the icy chill in Glenda's eyes.

"Because you need to know what's going on between us," she said.

"Oh?" Daniella asked, shifting her gaze to Glenda.

Glenda held out her ring finger. "Brent and I are engaged," she announced.

Shock twisted at Daniella's heart. *Calm down,* she thought.

"Congratulations," Daniella said, forcing a smile.

"Are you trying to tell me that you are happy for us?" Glenda asked.

Daniella shrugged. What did Glenda want her to do, have a seizure? Daniella drew in a deep breath and let it out slowly. Why Glenda was informing her of her and Brant's engagement was beyond her. "I have no reason not to wish you well," Daniella replied.

"Good. Because if you have any intentions of sinking your claws into my man, forget it," Glenda snapped.

Oh no she did not go there, Daniella thought, placing her hands on her hips.

"Look, I work with Brant and I'm not about to stop communicating with him because you're insecure," Daniella said.

"I'm not insecure," Glenda lashed out at Daniella.

"You're not, huh?" Daniella looked at her.

"No, I'm not," Glenda said, laughing.

"Then explain to me why it's so important to you that I stay away from him?" Daniella cocked her head and waited for an answer.

"Daniella whether you know it or not, I know that you and Brant were once lovers," Glenda pointed a finger at Daniella.

"I don't think you were back from Florida two weeks before you were working at Parker's Art again." Glenda's voice rose a level.

"Do you have a problem with that?" Daniella asked.

"No, but I do have a problem with you being his assistant!"

"And who told you that?"

"Honey, this is a small town."

"Excuse me, but I don't get it. What does being Brant's assistant have to do with this?" Daniella asked Glenda, eyeing her suspiciously.

"Aren't you assuming Tyrone's position?" Glenda asked.

"Of course."

"Which means that you'll be traveling with Brant," Glenda stated.

"Right, and your point is?" Daniella inquired.

"If you think that I am crazy enough to believe that you and Brant will sit around discussing designs, sugar, you better think again," Glenda said staring at Daniella.

"Answer this question for me Glenda. If Brant loves you, why are you worried about me?" Daniella inquired, and waited for a reply.

"Me—worried? I don't think I have to worry about a woman who couldn't keep her husband," Glenda shot back.

Daniella's face felt hot. Tears stung her eyes. She blinked. "My personal life is none of your business."

"Really?" Glenda smirked.

"Really. So, why would you marry a man that you don't trust?" Daniella watched as Glenda opened and closed her mouth as if she were unable to speak.

"I. . .we. . .I trust him."

"Then why are you here?"

"Because I don't trust you!" Glenda said.

"Child, please," Daniella said, holding up her hands.

The girls returned from their break and went to put on their dance shoes.

"Daniella, I'm sorry that your plans didn't materialize," Glenda said.

Daniella inhaled and slowly exhaled. "I have a class to teach," she said in a hushed tone. "Excuse me." She turned her attention to her aspiring dancers.

"Okay girls, let's move it," Daniella said, turning on the music. She glanced at Glenda. "Please leave. I'm busy."

For the rest of the evening, Daniella struggled to keep her mind free of Brant and his engagement to Glenda. But she didn't care if Brant was engaged to the Queen of Sheba's sister, nothing and no one was going to stand in the way of her building a friendship with her boss. She had plans to get her interior design job back and that was all there was to it, she thought.

CHAPTER 6

It was already after ten o'clock on Friday night when Brant took his luggage off the conveyer belt at Newark International Airport and headed out to his pickup. He wondered if Daniella was awake. He could hardly work for thinking about her while he was in North Carolina.

Brant turned the air conditioner on and stuck a jazz disc into the player. The music floated out, filling the truck's cab, bringing more thoughts of Daniella to mind. He wanted her. How he was going to change Daniella's mind about being his platonic friend was a different subject.

For starters, he'd finally made Glenda realize that their relationship was over.

The day Brant left for North Carolina, he'd stopped by Glenda's boutique in the mall and marched her down to the jewelry store so she could get a refund for the gold chain she'd bought for him. Now all he had to do was pursue Daniella. She had made the first move by inviting him to dinner. Brant tapped his chin with his forefinger. He would take things from there. He turned his truck onto the freeway and headed toward home.

The eagle on the gray Budweiser building flapped its red-neon wings as Brant weaved in and out of traffic heading back to Forest. The logo reminded him how surprised he was when he saw Daniella drinking a beer. But there was a lot that he didn't know about Daniella.

Like why was she in such a funk about dating after her divorce. Brant was going to find out why, he decided, pressing his foot against the gas pedal and changing lanes.

Brant had to admit that he was surprised when Daniella hadn't stayed upset with him for assigning her another job. Maybe, he had a chance with her after all, he thought, pulling up to the toll booth. He flipped a token in the container and sped off with memories of that night he had stopped unexpectedly by Daniella's town house weighing on his mind.

The subtle scent of Daniella's perfume had stayed with him most of that night. He would always remember how she felt in his arms that night he had gone to her home from the company's picnic years ago. She was not too hard and not too soft. Although he hadn't held Daniella since that night some years ago, her physical attributes didn't seem to have changed.

But a few nights ago, he had wanted to take Daniella in his arms and hold her when he realized how disappointed she was when she learned that they weren't going to Atlanta. He had wanted to comfort her, assure her that Georgia was a nice state to visit. But he didn't do that, and Daniella had been polite because he was her boss.

Brant jug-handled onto his exit. It wasn't long before he was turning onto Daniella's street, driving slow. When he noticed that the lights were off and the garage door closed, he assumed that she had gone to bed. He sped up and headed home, passing the community center. As usual, the lights were on in the building and the parking lot was filled with automobiles. Brant slowed and pulled over when he saw Daniella's Jeep parked in front. Before he could open the door, he saw her walk out of the building with Jerry. They stopped at the bottom of the steps. Brant watched Jerry cover Daniella's hand with his.

Jealousy raked Brant's insides like a hot pitchfork. He leaned back against the truck's seat and watched Daniella and Jerry. It was his fault that he had assumed that Daniella was still in love with her ex-husband.

Tomorrow night, I'm going to find out everything I can about the gorgeous Miss Taylor, Brant thought, pushing the truck's gear into first, moving down the street.

That night, Brant didn't sleep much. Around midnight, he couldn't stand his insomnia any longer. He called Tyrone.

"Yeah," Tyrone's voice was groggy, as if Brant had awakened him from a deep sleep.

"Tyrone, I hate to wake you, man, but I need to talk."

"I'm awake, what's up?"

"Did Dannie invite you and Beverly to a party tomorrow night?" Brant asked.

"You woke me up for that?" Tyrone asked, chuckling.

"Did she?" Branted wanted to know.

"Yeah," Tyrone said sounding as if he were yawning.

"I need a favor," Brant said, going into details about what he wanted Tyrone to do for him.

"I don't know Brant. Beverly is already mad at me," Tyrone said in a low voice, as if he didn't want to wake his wife.

"You owe me man," Brant said, reminding Tyrone of the time he'd worked all night completing one of Tyrone's projects so Tyrone could take Beverly to a Broadway show.

"What's wrong, Tyrone?" Brant heard Beverly say in the background.

"Nothing." Brant heard Tyrone say.

"So, are you going to help me out, or what?" Brant asked, after Tyrone had convinced Beverly that he was having a casual phone conversation with his best buddy.

"I'll think of something Brant," Tyrone said.

"Thanks guy." Brant hung up.

Finally, Brant dozed off. He slept and dreamed that he was holding Daniella close to him, pressing her round hips against him. She returned his kisses one after another with hungry passion, sending them both rocking and reeling out of control. Like the ending of a movie scene, Brant's dream faded to black. Brant jolted upright in bed. The digital clock on his nightstand flashed two o'clock. He laid back and rested his arm across his forehead. It was too late to call Daniella. He visualized her and Jerry holding hands. The picture made the nerves in his stomach coil into tight knots.

Unable to sleep, Brant got up and went downstairs to the kitchen. He poured a glass of spring water from the jug in the refrigerator, took his cordless phone off the cradle, and went out to the deck.

Brant punched in the number to his voice mail and listened to his messages.

"Brant this is your mother," Clara Parker's voice came across the line. "Boy, if you don't take a break from work, you're going to make yourself sick. Nick stopped by yesterday and he told me that you were working until all hours of the night." Brant's mother sounded worried. Brant groaned. He wished his brother would mind his own business.

When the message ended, Brant pushed the button and listened to the other messages. The next message was silent. Brant didn't have a clue who would waste their time calling him and not leaving a message. His next and final message was from Glenda. "Why're you so stubborn. You know as well as I do that we're good together." There was a pause in her message. "How many times do I have to say I'm sorry? Call me."

Brant pushed the button on the phone and set it on the table. He dropped down on the chaise lounge, drank the water, and thought about Daniella. She was the sweetest woman he had ever known. She had gotten away from him once. It won't happen again, he decided, draining his water glass.

CHAPTER 7

Saturday morning, after running a few errands, Daniella sat in her kitchen sipping iced coffee, while listening to the messages on her voice mail. The first message was from her mother announcing that her parents were back from the Bahamas sooner than they'd expected.

Daniella deleted the message, and made a mental note to call her parents over the weekend. The next message was from Beverly.

"Dannie, this is Beverly, I'm sorry, but Tyrone and I can't come to your dinner party tonight. Tyrone's half-brother and his wife came from New York and they're spending the weekend with us. I hope your dinner goes well. We'll talk," Beverly said.

"Doggone it!" Daniella lamented after hearing Beverly's message. She didn't know how she was going to keep Brant distracted from prying into her personal life. *I'll change the subject,* Daniella thought, pressing the number one, erasing the message. She hung up and called Beverly.

On the fourth ring, Beverly answered the phone.

"Beverly," Daniella said in a slow, even voice, as if Beverly had a problem understanding her.

"Yes, good morning and how are you," Beverly said, in a cheerful voice.

"I was fine until I got your message," Daniella said. "I thought Tyrone and his half-brother couldn't stand each other." Daniella asked.

Beverly laughed. "Oh girl, let me tell you. Tyrone called Bill this morning and they decided that it would be nice to get along for the sake of the children."

"That's nice," Daniella said dryly.

"So Tyrone invited Bill and his wife over for the weekend."

"Really." Daniella stated. From what Beverly had told her, it had been almost a year since Tyrone had spoken to his half-brother.

"Dannie, I get the feeling that you don't believe me," Beverly said.

"As a matter of fact, I don't," Daniella said, feeling betrayed by her best friend.

"Now, Dannie, you know how Tyrone is about family. He wants T.J. to know all of his cousins."

"I understand that," Daniella said, twisting the ends of her hair.

"I knew you would, Dannie," Beverly replied.

"I'm still not sure about you, Beverly," Daniella said, recalling when she first returned to New Jersey after her divorce. Beverly and Tyrone invited her to go to the art museum. Beverly had also invited her cousin Carl. At the last minute, Beverly and Tyrone

had an emergency and couldn't go. Daniella and Carl
had gone to the museum without them. Carl was
polite, well-mannered, and a perfect gentleman. However, in spite of it all, Daniella wasn't interested in
Carl's discussion on marriage and how he was looking
for a good wife.

Beverly laughed. "Don't tell me that you're going
to cancel the dinner party," Beverly inquired.

"Are you kidding, I spent too many evenings per-
fecting the meal. Besides that, my goal is to make
Brant my pal," Daniella reminded her girlfriend.

"I heard that." Beverly giggled.

"All right, girl, I'll talk to you later. I have a million
and ten things to do." Daniella said good-bye and
hung up.

Daniella went upstairs and got her purse. She
peered in the dresser's mirror and checked her
makeup. The baggy jumpsuit she wore was comfortable, just right for grocery shopping. She hurried
downstairs and went next door to Grace Mills, leaving
her house key with the woman so that the Brushes
and Broom cleaning service could get inside to clean
her house while she grocery-shopped for her dinner
party.

Several hours later, the aroma of baked apples mingled with spicy brown chicken floated from Daniella's
opened kitchen window. Daniella took the chilled
bottle of white wine from the refrigerator and popped
the cork so the vintage beverage could breathe. She
set the table with her bone china. Before Daniella
set the *acini di pepe* fruit pudding on the counter to
cool, she tasted the dessert.

"Hmmm, that's good," she said, putting the spoon in the dishwasher. She took the dinner rolls from the oven and set them in the warmer, then turned the oven down low so the chicken could finish baking for a few more minutes.

All that was left to cook was the broccoli, which Daniella decided to steam just before Brant arrived for dinner. She filled a long-stemmed wineglass with Chablis to take with her to sip while she soaked in a warm bubblebath.

Daniella went upstairs to the bathroom and filled the tub with hot water and cherry-scented bubblebath. While she waited for the tub to fill, she went to the kitchen for the glass of wine she'd forgotten.

By the time she returned to the bathroom, the tub was filled with warm water and soft, thick white bubbles. She took several pink sponge rollers from the vanity and set her hair. Daniella discarded her clothes, and stepped into the tub.

As she sipped the wine and soaked in her warm bubblebath, Daniella allowed herself to think of Brant Parker. When she was around Brant, her heart fluttered and sometimes, she even felt giddy, like a teenage girl. What was worse than her feelings, was the fact that she had no control over them. Daniella took another sip of wine. *It's a pity Brant is getting married,* she mused, setting the glass down on the edge of the tub. If only she could trust men, Brant would've been the perfect guy for her, Daniella decided, closing her eyes, visualizing his handsome face, and strong muscular body. He was also practical: He worked hard and in most cases he was kind of nice. Daniella concluded her evaluation of Brant Parker.

However, Brant was a tough guy when it came to

business. Daniella knew that from working with him years ago. Brant's father had left him in charge of Parker's Art one summer. Daniella, Beverly, and a few others were working to complete the decoration of an exclusive downtown hotel. They had worked hard, but as fate would have it, they were confronted with one complication after another.

Nonetheless, Daniella remembered that Brant had made her and the other designers work all hours of the night to complete the project. Daniella had thought she would drop in her tracks from exhaustion. Not once did she think that Brant had made them work just to prove that he was in control. She was sure of it, since the project was completed a day ahead of schedule. Daniella quickly dismissed the annoying memories from her mind and finished her wine before stepping out of the tub.

All she had to do tonight was stay cool and in control of her and Brant's conversation. Daniella shook her head. She wasn't going to fool herself for one moment. She knew she'd chosen a powerful opponent.

Daniella draped the towel around her and went to her bedroom. After she applied lotion, sprinkled powder, and dabbed on perfume, she sat at her vanity and applied her makeup just so.

Daniella often wore her hair twisted in a loose bun. For some reason she thought the hairstyle gave her a serious business appearance. But tonight, she wanted to appear friendly and carefree, she decided, removing the pink rollers and brushing her hair until the curls were soft and bouncy, sweeping around her shoulders.

Daniella slipped into the silk tan summer dress and

stuck her feet into a pair of two-inch heels that looked as if they were made of glass.

The gentle sound of a diesel motor sent Daniella to her bedroom balcony door just in time to see Brant's black Mercedes pull up behind her Jeep.

Daniella straightened the bottles of perfume on her dresser and smoothed the comforter on her bed. By the time she finished doing that, the doorbell rang. She hurried downstairs and took one final glance at herself in the mirror near the stairway before opening the door for Brant.

Daniella's gaze shifted slowly over Brant. His dark blue suit, light blue silk shirt, and black wing-tipped shoes made him look as if he'd stepped out of a men's fashion magazine.

"Hi," Brant spoke, holding out a dozen red roses to her.

Daniella smiled and spoke, taking the flowers from Brant. His broad fingers touched hers, sending unwanted shivers through her. *Oh my God, help me to get through this night,* Daniella silently whispered.

"Thank you," she said. "Come in." She moved aside so that he could walk into her living room. He moved with assurance and ease as he crossed over to the sofa, and sat, crossing his legs in a figure four.

Brant's mouth curved into a smile. "How have you been?" he asked, settling back against the soft cushions.

"I'm fine. How was your trip?" Daniella inquired as if she were interested in discussing the completed work noted on her architectural Punch sheets.

"Everything went well," Brant replied.

Daniella moved toward the kitchen. "I'll get you a

glass of wine while I finish dinner," she said, referring to the broccoli that needed steaming.

"All right." Brant got up, following Daniella to the kitchen.

"You don't have to come with me. I'll be right back," she said, wishing Brant would stay in the living room.

"I'd rather be with you." He grinned, pulling back a stool, sitting at the counter while Daniella took a vase from the cabinet, filled it with water, and stuck the roses in it.

After Daniella had set the flowers in the center of her dining room table, she took a chilled wineglass from the freezer and set it before Brant.

"Help yourself," she said, pointing to the wine on the counter.

"Thanks," Brant said, filling his glass with Chablis.

Daniella put the broccoli in the steamer and turned the range's eye on high, and gasped.

"Lord have mercy Jesus!" Daniella's hand flew to her chest.

"What?" Brant asked, swinging around on the stool, glancing from Daniella to the oven.

"I—I forgot to take the chicken out of the oven," she said in a strained voice, opening the oven door to check the meat. She took a fork from the drawer and stuck it lightly into the gourmet chicken, testing it for tenderness.

Needless to say, the overcooked bird was as tough as leather.

"Oooh," Daniella uttered under her breath.

"Are you all right?" Brant asked, setting his glass down, going over to stand beside her.

"No, I'm not all right. Dinner is ruined," Daniella

confessed, embarrassed and hurt that she had schemed hard to make Brant her friend with her cooking and now he was going to think that she couldn't boil water without scorching it. She removed the roaster from the oven and set it on the counter.

"Don't worry about it, we'll go out and eat," Brant offered.

"Only if I pay," Daniella said, avoiding Brant's gaze.

"I'm buying dinner, and that's all there is to it," Brant said.

"But I invited you here," Daniella replied.

"So, I'm inviting you to dinner," Brant said. "Let's go."

Daniella turned the stove off and removed the half-steamed broccoli from the eye and put the vegetable in the refrigerator. She had no one to blame but herself for this fine mess. She hated it when men offered to buy anything for her. Ray had been the generous type and look what happened to her." Daniella recalled her marriage to Ray as she went for her purse.

Seconds later, she was downstairs.

"I'm ready," she said to Brant, who was standing near the door waiting for her. "I'm really sorry about dinner, Brant," Daniella apologized, while they walked to his car.

"Ah, it's all right," Brant replied, chuckling while unlocking the passenger's door and opening it for Daniella.

Daniella slid in, wishing Brant would stop trying to impress her with male etiquette. It wasn't necessary for him to open doors for her, she thought as she watched him walk around to the other side of the car.

"Where would you like to go for dinner?" Brant asked, sliding in beside her.

For a few seconds, Daniella was undecided. The Café was too noisy on a Saturday night, and Omar's was even worse with the noise.

"Let's go to the Glow," Daniella said, glancing at Brant.

"All right," Brant said, turning on the headlights and backing out of the driveway.

Daniella settled back against the soft, black leather seat listening to the jazz that piped through the speakers and thanked her lucky stars that she wasn't a betting woman. If anyone would've told her that Brant would be taking her out to dinner tonight, she would've lost fair and square.

Daniella made small conversation about things that had happened at work while he was in North Carolina. She decided it would be better for her to wait before she congratulated him on his engagement to Glenda. Such intimate details would be best left for him to discuss.

While Daniella talked shop, she noticed that Brant was quieter than usual. He answered her questions with a "yes," or "no." She figured that he wasn't talking much because he was probably tired. *Good,* Daniella mused, thinking how nice her evening was turning out. She wouldn't have to worry about him questioning her past. On top of that, it wasn't like they were out on a real date. The man was engaged for crying out loud.

Nevertheless, the soft rumbling of Brant's quick answers was making Daniella's heart flutter and her face warm.

"Will you turn the air conditioner up?" Daniella

asked, realizing that they were close to the restaurant, but if she didn't get some air, she didn't know what would happen to her.

Brant gave Daniella a side glance, while changing the temperature.

Five minutes later, they parked in The Glow's parking lot. Brant got out and walked around to open the door for Daniella.

But before he could reach the passenger's side of the car, Daniella had opened the door and stepped out onto the parking lot.

"You know, Dannie, I've been watching you."

Daniella shot Brant a cool glance. "Really," she said walking beside him.

"Yeah, do you have a problem with men being polite to you, or is it me?" Brant looked at her.

"What do you mean?" she asked, as if she didn't know what he was talking about.

"I offered to buy dinner and you refused. I like opening doors for my woman and you. . ."

"Your woman?" Daniella asked meeting his gaze, remembering that Brant was engaged.

Brant slipped his arm around her waist while they walked to restaurant.

"We'll talk," he said, opening the restaurant's door so she could walk in before him.

"Which reminds me, I forgot to congratulate you on your engagement," Daniella said as they waited for the hostess to seat them. Maybe, Brant needed reminding.

A strange, intense look flashed in Brant's eyes.

"What did you say?" Brant stepped back and looked at Daniella.

"Oh please, don't tell me that you forgot a thing

like that." Daniella said when the hostess came over
and led them to a table in a cozy section near the
back.

As they moved between rows of tables covered with
white silk cloths, Daniella glanced around the room
at the well-dressed couples seated at the tables, carrying on quiet conversations and sipping wine.

Brant pulled back a chair for Daniella and waited
for her to sit. When she had settled down, Brant
walked around the table and sat across from her.

Brant picked up the wine list and studied it for a
while, then glanced at Daniella. "I think I misunderstood you when you said I was engaged," he said,
eyeing her closely.

"You heard me. But for the record, I was congratu-
lating you on your engagement," Daniella repeated,
glancing at the huge chandeliers that looked like
diamonds hanging from the ceiling.

Brant chuckled. "Who told you that?"

"Are you denying that you're engaged?" Daniella
answered his inquiry with a question.

Brant dropped the wine list and leaned back in the
chair, resting his hands on the arms of the chair.

"When I get in engaged, you'll be the first to
know," Brant said.

Daniella had avoided Brant's gaze until she
couldn't. It seemed that his light brown eyes burned
her, forcing her to return and hold his glance.

"Okay. . .if it's a rumor, I'm sorry that I repeated
it." Daniella shifted in her chair.

The waiter came over and took their food and wine
orders, relieving Daniella of the pressure to continue
any conversation with Brant about his personal life.

When the waiter left their table, Brant cleared his

throat. "So, what happened to make you divorce the guy?" Brant asked, as if it were his business to know. Daniella's eyes widened with surprise. "You get right to the point, don't you?" Daniella asked, undecided about whether she should answer Brant's question.

"I'm asking." Brant's voice surprised Daniella even more.

"Why do you want to know?" Daniella's voice rose over the quiet laughter and conversations.

"Because I want to ask you something, and I need to know just where I stand with you," Brant said.

"I don't understand what my divorce has to do with what you want to ask me," Daniella said, casting Brant an uncomfortable glance.

Once again, the waiter came to the rescue, setting the wine on the table before them.

"Thanks," Daniella said to the young man, and smiled. She immediately took a sip of the white wine, and hoped that Brant would stop prying into that part of her life that she wanted to forget.

"What I have to ask you has everything to do with your past, Dannie," Brant said.

Daniella set her glass down and decided to play along with Brant.

"What do you want to know other than why I divorced my ex-husband?" Daniella asked nonchalantly.

Brant reached back and rubbed the back of his neck.

"Where is he?" Brant inquired, holding her gaze.

Brant's question didn't surprise Daniella at all, since he'd hinted over the phone the night she called him that he was interested in her personal life. At first she'd thought he was interested in her, but after talking to Glenda, Daniella thought she knew better.

"He's dead. Are you satisfied?" Daniella asked, lifting her wineglass to her lips, enjoying the white vintage.

"Not really," Brant replied.

"Then what do you want me to say?" Daniella cast Brant a cool glance.

"It's not impossible that you can still love him, even after he's dead," Brant said.

Daniella set the wineglass down hard, making sprinkles of wine splash from the glass. "Brant, please, I don't want to discuss this." She despised Ray Spencer for all the things he had done to her and Brant was sitting there imagining her having undying love for Ray.

The waiter set their food on the table. Annoyed at Brant, Daniella forced herself to smile at the waiter and spread her napkin on her lap while the young man fussed over them to make sure they enjoyed their meal.

"So I'm right, you do still love him," Brant said, after the waiter had left them.

A nervous knot coiled in Daniella's stomach. The best way to handle this conversation was to act as if it never took place, she thought, cutting into the jumbo shrimp, spearing it with her fork, and putting the tender meat in her mouth. She chewed slowly, trying to think of something other than Ray Spencer to discuss.

"How's your father?" Daniella asked.

Brant looked up from cutting into the New York strip and laid his fork and knife down.

"He's fine, and don't change the subject."

Daniella placed her fork on her plate and looked out the window. Why Brant insisted on discussing her personal life was beyond her.

"No, I don't love Ray," Daniella replied, hoping to end the trail of questions Brant was firing at her.

"It's been a while since your divorce, and I've noticed that you don't have a man friend. . .unless you're dating Jerry," Brant said, gazing at Daniella intensely.

"What is this, twenty questions?" Daniella wound a strand of spaghetti around her fork.

Brant's eyes narrowed. "Are you seeing Jerry?"

Daniella held her fork, frozen midair. "Why?" she asked before she continued to eat.

"I'm curious," Brant replied, attacking his steak.

"It's none of your business, but no. Jerry and I are friends," Daniella answered him, hoping this was the last round of questions.

"What kind of friends?" Brant wanted to know.

"My God, you ask a lot of questions Brant, "Daniella said.

"I want to know," he remarked.

Daniella ignored Brant's question, and continued to eat the spaghetti marinara.

"Dannie, I'm waiting for an answer," Brant glanced at her.

Daniella laid her fork down and sat back in her chair.

"Jerry and I are platonic friends," she stated evenly.

Brant leaned forward and looked out into the dining room.

"Oh, I understand," he replied. "You have lots of platonic friends—huh?"

Oh my lord, Daniella thought. She had asked Brant

for his friendship and now he was probably thinking that she was playing a game with him. With that thought in mind, Daniella decided it was best that she answer his questions as honestly as possible and find out what questions he wanted to ask her from the beginning.

"Jerry and I are childhood friends. Now, what did you want to ask me earlier?" Daniella asked, reaching for her wine, taking a sip.

"Will you be my lady?" Brant asked Daniella.

The wine went down her throat the wrong way. "Ahhhhh," Daniella slapped her chest with her free hand.

Brant hurried around to her and began patting her back as if she was a small child that needed assistance.

"Are you all right, Dannie?" Brant asked, squatting beside her chair.

Daniella cleared her throat and wiped the strangled tears from her eyes with her napkin.

"I'm fine," she said, after composing herself. "But I can't do that," she said.

"Why not?" Brant asked her, still stroking her back.

"Listen, Brant, I don't think I have the energy to get involved in a relationship right now," she stated, as Brant rose from his squat and went to his chair.

"All right. I think I can understand that. But with you, Dannie, it's all or nothing." Brant drained his wineglass and set the goblet down.

"I thought that since we worked together, we could have more than a boss and employee relationship," Daniella said, hoping Brant would agree with her.

Instead of replying to Daniella's suggestion, Brant signaled for the waiter that was standing nearby.

Daniella stared at Brant, realizing the shocking fact:

Brant wasn't engaged to Glenda, which meant he was a free man. And to complicate matters worse, he'd asked her to be his lady. Daniella reached for her purse. She wasn't ready for an intimate relationship.

"I have to get out of here," she said, pushing away from the table.

"Dannie," Brant called after her.

Daniella heard him, but she didn't look back. She reached into her purse, took out her cellular phone and called a cab. Her plans had gone awry. Brant was asking her for more than she could give. She had lost all trust in the affairs of the heart. How could he put her on the spot like that? she thought while waiting for the cab.

It wasn't long before Brant was beside her. He slipped his arms around Daniella's waist and drew her close.

"I brought you here and I'm taking you home," he said, drawing her close. Slowly, his lips touched hers. Daniella felt her legs weaken as he gathered her closer.

"I need to think, Brant," Daniella said.

"About what, us?" His breath was hot against her lips.

Daniella sank against his muscular chest.

"Yes," she said, trying to find the strength to tear out of his embrace. *Get away from this man,* she told herself, unable to control the mass of passionate emotions that raked at her heart.

Brant caressed Daniella's face with a soft gaze before he lowered his head farther, claiming her lips with a burning kiss that left her swirling and tingling. Without thinking, she returned his kisses freely.

Suddenly, Brant pulled away, and held Daniella at arm's length.

"Let's go," he said, walking with her to his car.

Daniella silently agreed while calling to cancel the taxi.

Again, they were quiet as Brant drove her home. Every once in a while, Daniella stole a glance at him out of the corner of her eye. She thought that she had no passionate feelings left inside her until Brant kissed her tonight. His kiss was like hot brandy on a cold winter's night, melting the ice from her soul. Daniella's passion had been lit and was threatening to grow into a roaring fire. She needed time to think. It was all happening too fast.

Minutes later, Brant parked in Daniella's driveway. He cut off the lights and motor on his Mercedes, and turned to her, draping his arm across the top of the car seat.

"I can't pretend that I don't want you, Dannie," Brant said, eyeing her with an intense gaze. "I understand that you may not be ready to love me. But I can wait."

Daniella glanced at Brant. He could wait? He'd just walked into her life and unleashed every ounce of scorching desire in her and he understood her reservations?

"Good night, Brant, and thanks for dinner," she said, reaching for the door handle.

Brant reached out and took her hand. He opened his door, got out, and pulled Daniella behind him.

"Good night," Brant said, after Daniella unlocked her door. He slipped his arms around her waist, squeezing her to him, planting feather kisses on her lips.

"I'll see you later," Brant said, releasing his grasp on her.

Daniella went inside, closed the door, and dropped down on the sofa. *Lord what have I done?* she wondered. Suddenly, the room seemed to close in around Daniella. She had to get out, go for a drive. It didn't matter where, as long as she was out of the house.

Daniella grabbed her purse and turned out all the lights except her bedroom and living room lamp lights. She got into her Jeep and started riding.

CHAPTER 8

Brant pressed the brakes, slowing the Mercedes as he drove down the dimly lit road going to his lake house. Pitch pines and red oaks rose over the black pavement like giants in the middle of the night. His thoughts wandered to Daniella as he adjusted the air conditioner to a lower level. He couldn't stop thinking about her, and for that reason, he couldn't sleep. So he drove out to his house on the lake to check on the repairs that James had completed.

Brant turned on the radio. Music usually kept him from worrying. But tonight, the sound of jazz floating from the speakers of the radio made him think about Daniella more.

Even after he explained his feelings for her, Daniella had rejected him.

Then, to make matters worse, he had gone and done exactly what he had promised himself he wouldn't do. He had lost control and kissed her. Brant gripped the steering wheel. He could give her the interior design job, but she would think she had won. A wry smile played around Brant's mouth. He was no fool, he knew exactly what that dinner was all about. He had to thank Tyrone for helping him out tonight. Only a good friend like Tyrone would invite a half-brother he could barely stand over for the weekend, just so his buddy could stake his claim on a woman he wanted. However, Daniella didn't want him, at least not yet, Brant mused. But, he was a patient man, and he knew from experience that timing was everything.

Brant parked at the curve of his house at the lake. A fresh coat of sandalwood varnish scented the midnight air. The walkway had been repaired and painted gray. From the streetlight sitting at the edge of Brant's property, he could see that the brown patches in the grass were turning green. A flower bed mixed with blue mist spiraea, river birch, hollyhocks, and bachelor's buttons made a multicolored trail to the steps of the house.

Brant observed James Amour's handiwork, and decided that he hadn't made a bad choice in giving the guy a job at repairing his property after all.

The house was dark and quiet, an indication that James was out. He was probably just leaving his janitor's job at the gym, Brant thought, turning his key in the lock. The scent of more fresh paint and new wood floated over Brant.

Large, white square tiles covered the living room floor. The sofa that had come with the house was covered with a dusty sheet. James hadn't gotten around to throwing out the two stools. Brant turned

on the lights and took the bottle of twelve-year-old
Scotch that George had given him the day of the
closing from the bar's cabinet and set it on the top
of the bar. He noticed the bottle was half full. James
must have helped himself to the liquor, Brant
thought.

Apparently James also spent a lot of time repairing
the house. The kitchen cabinets that Brant ordered
were installed as well as the stove and the refrigerator.
On the table were power tools and in the center of
the floor lay a ladder and iron pipe. Brant picked up
an empty paint bucket and carried it outside to the
garbage bin.

The lake was the place he had wanted Daniella to
see. It had always filled him with serenity. When he
needed to think, Brant came to the lake. Tonight,
he had made the short trip, hoping that he could
forget Daniella's rejection. He should've known better, he mused, dropping the paint bucket in the bin
and moving over to the rim of the lake. He took off
his jacket and laid it on a rock, then propped one
foot on the edge of the stone and gazed out at the
water. A small silver boat tied to the pier rocked back
and forth against the waves.

Tired of standing, Brant pushed his jacket aside
and sat on the large rock, crossing his legs Indian
style, allowing his mind to wander, savoring the satis-
faction of holding Daniella tonight. It wasn't that he
wasn't used to women. God knows he'd had more
than his share. Bed-hopping was what his brother
Nick had accused him of doing for years until lately.
Brant hadn't agreed. Most of his dates had been fun
and nothing more.

Before he graduated from college, Brant had wooed the ladies with his natural charm and charisma.

After Brant graduated from college and his dad finally gave him a position traveling for Parker's Art, Brant was in lovers' heaven. He could've had a woman in every state, but he didn't.

The years slipped passed and community health became an important world issue. He was as healthy as a horse, and planned to stay that way. So he and Glenda chose each other for lovers. She was an independent one-man woman, and he'd liked that about her. Brant and Glenda worked out a plan. When Brant wasn't traveling, he spent most his nights with Glenda. He gave her expensive gifts and treated her almost as if she were his wife.

In return, Glenda showered Brant with her affection. Brant thought their relationship was perfect until Glenda insisted that she and Brant should get married.

Brant had been ambivalent to marriage. However, he and Glenda could've settled down into a semi-happy state of matrimony if she weren't so jealous. Insecure, Brant mused. Glenda had also lied to him about being pregnant. The woman was crazy. She was like a clinging vine, wrapping herself around him, suffocating his mind, body, and soul. Brant loved his freedom and that was one of the reasons he'd left her.

But now, for the first time in his life, he was gung ho over a woman. Daniella. He didn't want to be free of her. He would marry Daniella tonight if she would have him. It was clear that she didn't want any part of him. Or did she? Brant reflected on how she had kissed him tonight.

Music playing in the distance drew Brant out of his thoughts. He stood up, took his jacket from the rock, and followed the sound. About five houses down, someone was throwing a party.

The closer Brant got to the house, the louder the music and voices got. He could smell charcoal and barbecue sauce, seafood, and frying chicken.

Before Brant could get into the yard, a woman he had met a few years back, walked up to him, grabbing his arm. Brant glanced at her, trying to remember her name.

"Well, if it's not Brant Parker," the woman said, giving Brant a seductive smile.

Brant shifted his gaze to the attractive woman, raising his brow a fraction of an inch, trying to recall where he had met her. Her khaki short-shorts and bra-length blouse exposed her narrow waist, accenting her figure. She removed her wide-brimmed safari hat, as if showing off her short scrunch hairstyle would click Brant's memory.

"Is this your party?" Brant asked her, still trying to figure out where he knew her from.

"No." She stepped in front of Brant and studied his face. "You don't remember me, do you?" the woman asked.

Brant shrugged and pushed his free hand in his pants' pocket. "No," he said, moving toward the house.

"Well, it doesn't matter, because by the end of the night, you will," the woman said, following Brant inside.

Brant's brother, Nick, was sitting at the bar, engaged in a conversation with Monique, the owner of Shagreen Aesthetic Salon.

"What's up, man?" Brant spoke to Nick.

"You got it, brother." Nick grinned.

Brant glanced at Monique, and nodded.

"Oh yeah, this is Monique McRay. Her family is a client of mine," Nick explained as if Brant was interested in whom he dated.

"I know." Brant glanced at Nick, a little surprised that he seemed to have been enjoying being with Monique. Brant knew his brother's situation. He hadn't seen Nick that interested in a woman since his divorce.

Nick looked at the woman standing next to Brant, then glanced at Brant.

"Oh, ah, what's your name, babe?" Brant asked the woman.

"I'm Evelyn, darling." She smiled at Brant.

"Right," Brant laughed and sat on a stool and ordered two drinks. How could he forget Evelyn, realizing that they'd met years ago on the cruise ship that Evelyn worked on. He had gone to the islands for a couple of weeks of vacation. Evelyn had gotten off the ship to shop and visit friends. Instead, she and Brant went out for dinner, dancing, and drinks. This was the first time Brant had seen Evelyn since that time. He couldn't believe she still remembered him.

"Are you still with the cruise line?" Brant asked, making conversation. He wished it was Daniella he was talking to instead of a woman he hardly knew.

"No, I work for the telephone company now," Evelyn replied.

Brant glanced at her.

"I know," Evelyn said, "But I got tired of the high seas. What can I say." She laughed.

"There's nothing wrong with that." Brant turned a bottle of seltzer water up to his mouth.

"Yeah, I settled down and bought one of those houses at the Carriage Place that your company designed," Evelyn said.

"I'm glad you're satisfied with it," Brant replied.

"Why don't you and I get out of here and go to my place," Evelyn suggested. "That way, you can see how nice my home is," she said, laughing.

Brant checked his watch. It was getting close to one o'clock in the morning. Besides, he didn't want to see a house that his company had designed. He had seen the houses more times than he cared to think about. Brant drained the bottle and stood up. So far talking to Evelyn had kept his mind off Daniella. However, he didn't feel like going home, knowing that he wouldn't be able to sleep.

"Let's go to The Café," Brant suggested. Years ago he may have gone home with Evelyn and most likely they would've spent the night talking and listening to music since he didn't know her that well. Nonetheless, from experience he knew that type of situation usually raised false hope.

"Okay," Evelyn agreed, pushing her way through the crowded room, pulling Brant along with her, as she searched for her girlfriend.

"Uh, uh, uh, what a knight in shining armor," Evelyn's girlfriend commented.

Brant groaned, ignoring the woman's admiration. The only woman he wanted to shine for was Daniella.

"I'll have to ride with you," Evelyn said to Brant. "I got a ride over here with my friend."

What have I gotten myself into now? Brant mused, having second thoughts about going dancing with

Evelyn. On the other hand, it was better to go to The Café with Evelyn than to go home to a big, empty house and lose sleep worrying about how he was going to make his next move on Daniella.

"All right," Brant said, as they headed out to his car.

The Café was crowded and cool. As usual, the room smelled like cigarette smoke. A live band was on the stage playing an instrumental interlude while the singer took a break.

Brant found a table for him and Evelyn, excused himself, and went to the bar to order drinks. As he pushed through the crowd and weaved around tables, he saw her, or at least he thought he did. Brant wasn't sure. Instead of going to the bar, Brant walked over to the edge of the bandstand and touched the woman's arm. Daniella swirled around.

"What're you doing out this late?" Brant leaned down and whispered in Daniella's ear to keep from yelling out his question over the music.

"I could ask you the same question," Daniella shot back.

"But Dannie . . ."

"But Dannie what—you're a man and I'm a woman. Is that the reason I'm supposed to stay home after midnight?" Daniella asked.

"No, it's dangerous out here," Brant said.

"Oh, now I understand your reason for bringing an escort with you." Daniella gave Brant a wicked smile. "You need protection at night."

"Ah Dannie, it's not like that . . . she . . . Oh, what the hell," Brant lamented. This was not his night. He glanced across the room at Evelyn who was sitting patiently waiting for him to return with their drinks.

He couldn't just leave the woman sitting there after he'd driven her to the club. "I'll be right back," Brant said to Daniella and pushed his way over to the table.

"Where are the drinks?" Evelyn asked, smiling at Brant.

"Ah, Evelyn I'm sorry, I ran into a friend and . . ."

Evelyn stood. "That's okay. You didn't expect to see her here tonight, did you?" She smiled.

Brant didn't have an answer to Evelyn's question.

"I can call a cab for you?" Brant insisted.

"Thanks, Brant," Evelyn said, as they walked out of The Café. "Maybe we can go dancing some other time." She smiled.

Brant was glad that Evelyn understood. He was in enough trouble as it was. Here he was trying to make Daniella his woman, and she'd seen him with Evelyn, a woman he barely knew and wasn't thinking about. He helped Evelyn into a taxi, gave the driver enough money to take care of what he thought the fare should be from The Café to the Carriage Place, and went to find Daniella.

The singer was back onstage. Brant crossed the room to the entertainer and made a request, asking the performer to sing one of his favorite love songs. The singer agreed.

Brant glanced around the crowded room for Daniella. He saw her and his secretary, Joyce, sitting at the table with a couple of other women. By the time Brant reached Daniella, the singer had begun singing Brant's requested song.

"Ladies," Brant spoke to the women at Daniella's table, then lowered his head to Daniella's ear, brushing his lips against her cheek.

"Can I have this dance?" Brant took Daniella's hand, pleased at the light moan that escaped her lips.

Daniella looked at him. "Yes," she said, rising from her seat, allowing Brant to lead her out onto the crowded dance floor.

"Brant Parker, did you know that men weren't allowed near this table?" Joyce asked her boss.

Brant laughed. "What is this, a secret club?"

"Honey, this is Ladies' Night Out," another woman said, laughing.

Brant stretched his arms wide and shrugged his broad shoulders. "Tonight, I'm breaking the rules," he said, chuckling under his breath.

When he and Daniella reached the center of the floor, Brant's smile faded. His expression became serious as he circled his arms around Daniella's waist and held her close. They barely moved to the slow melody. Oh what a night this is, Brant mused, lowering his head, again touching his lips to the side of Daniella's cheek. He felt her shiver. He raised his head and kissed her parted lips.

They didn't talk much. Dancing and holding each other seemed more important than words. Finally, around three o'clock in the morning, Brant and Daniella left the club.

"I'll follow you home," Brant said.

"Brant, I can get home without your help," Daniella said, covering her mouth, yawning.

Brant glanced at Daniella. Her eyes were red from lack of sleep. "I think I'll leave my car here and drive you home," Brant decided, ignoring Daniella's statement.

"I don't think that's a good idea," Daniella said.

Brant reached for her Jeep key. He and Daniella could dance all night, but when it came to them making a reasonable decision, they didn't seem to agree on anything. Brant took her keys and they walked slowly arm in arm to her Jeep.

On the ride home, Daniella laid her head on Brant's shoulder and dozed off. Having Daniella so close to him made Brant feel good. Maybe they were making some headway into a relationship. *God, if I'm dreaming, don't wake me,* Brant prayed, pulling into Daniella's driveway.

He kissed her lightly before he cut the engine and switched off the headlights.

"Come on, let's go inside," he said, opening the door and standing aside so Daniella could get out. He wanted to lift her in his arms and carry her inside. He wouldn't carry her inside for all the tea in China, unless he wanted to start Desert Storm, part two. One thing he had learned about Daniella. She was independent to the core of her being.

Once inside Daniella's town house, Brant watched her kick off her shoes and go up to her bedroom.

"Thanks, Brant," Daniella said. "If you want to call a cab, the phone is in the kitchen," she called down from the top of the stairs.

Brant pushed his hands in his pockets and went to call a cab. Before he picked up the receiver, the phone rang. He let the phone ring a few times, thinking that Daniella would get it. When she didn't, Brant answered the call.

"Hello," Brant said into the receiver.

A long, dark silence except for heavy breathing was

the only sound Brant heard from the other end of the line.

"Hello?" Brant repeated.

"If I were you, I'd keep a close eye on Daniella," the person's voice on the other end sounded as if it was rigged with some kind of mechanical device.

"Who is this?" Brant asked, when the caller slammed the receiver down.

Brant held the receiver in his hand for a second, before setting it back on the cradle. He went to the foot of the stairway, then changed his mind about going up to discuss the phone call with Daniella. He figured tomorrow would be a better time to talk to her. If she was in trouble, he wanted to know about it. Brant removed his jacket, shirt, and shoes, laying them on a nearby chair. He unsnapped his pants, and turned out the light and sank down on the sofa. Brant propped his head on a couple of Daniella's throw pillows, and got as comfortable as he could. After that threatening phone call, he felt that he should sleep over.

James Amour stumbled up the lake house steps. He wasn't sure of the time. It was early morning, he knew that much. Working on Brant Parker's house during the day and cleaning the gym at night was rough. Especially when he stopped at the bar after getting off at the gym on a Saturday night. He'd drunk too much cheap Scotch.

Soon, James thought, reflecting on his goals as he staggered up to the front door, fishing around in his trouser pocket for the key. *Soon, I'll have my debts paid*

An important message from the ARABESQUE Editor

Dear Arabesque Reader,

Because you've chosen to read one of our Arabesque romance novels, we'd like to say "thank you"! And, as a special way to thank you, we've selected two more of the books you love so well to send you absolutely FREE!

Please enjoy them with our compliments, and thank you for continuing to enjoy Arabesque...the soul of romance.

Karen R. Thomas

Karen Thomas
Senior Editor,
Arabesque Romance Novels

ARABESQUE

A PRODUCT OF

☆BET BOOKS

3 QUICK STEPS
TO RECEIVE YOUR FREE "THANK YOU" GIFT
FROM THE EDITOR

Send back this card and you'll receive 2 Arabesque novels—absolutely free! These books have a combined cover price of $10.00 or more, but they are yours to keep absolutely free.

There's no catch. You're under no obligation to buy anything. We charge nothing for the books—ZERO—for your 2 free books (except $1.50 for shipping and handling). And you don't have to make any minimum number of purchases—not even one!

We hope that after receiving your free books you'll want to remain an Arabesque subscriber. But the choice is yours to continue or cancel, anytime at all! So why not take us up on our invitation to receive your free gift, with no risk of any kind. You'll be glad you did!

FREE BOOK CERTIFICATE

Yes! Please send me 2 free Arabesque books. I understand I am under no obligation to purchase any books, as explained on the back of this card.

Name _____

Address _____ Apt. _____

City_____ State_____ Zip_____

Telephone ( ) _____

Signature _____

Offer limited to one per household and not valid to current subscribers. All orders subject to approval. Terms, offer, & price subject to change.

Thank you!

AB0699

Accepting the two introductory free books places you under no obligation to buy anything. You may keep the books and return the shipping statement marked "cancel". If you do not cancel, about a month later we will send 4 additional Arabesque novels, and bill you a preferred subscriber's price of just $4.00 per title (plus a small shipping and handling fee). That's $16.00 for all 4 books for a saving of 25% off the publisher's price. You may cancel at any time, but if you choose to continue, every month we'll send you 4 more books, which you may either purchase at the preferred discount price. . .or return to us and cancel your subscription.

THE ARABESQUE ROMANCE CLUB
c/o ZEBRA HOME SUBSCRIPTION SERVICE, INC.
120 BRIGHTON ROAD
P.O. BOX 5214
CLIFTON, NEW JERSEY 07015-5214

AFFIX
STAMP
HERE

off and I can get out of this town. James pulled the key from his pocket and unlocked the front door.

Groaning, he staggered inside, taking two steps forward and one backward until he reached the bedroom. He fell across the bed, dozing off in a drunken stupor.

CHAPTER 9

Sunday around noon, Daniella laid in her bed inhaling the scent of fresh-brewed coffee and soaking up the yellow strands of sun rays that shone through her bedroom window. While enjoying her morning in bed, thoughts of her night with Brant came to mind.

First of all, why had she allowed him to kiss her? Added to that thought came the fact that she had enjoyed Brant's kiss and to make matters worse, she had kissed him back. Hadn't she promised herself that she was going to stay clear of a romantic relationship? The simple truth was, she didn't know what she was going to do about her situation with Brant. However, they were both adults and once she explained her reasons for not wanting to play love games with him, her and Brant's situation would dissolve.

The scent of coffee grew stronger as Daniella got

out of bed and went to the bathroom for her shower. Usually, Grace Mills was in church this time of day, Daniella thought, turning the shower nozzle and stepping into the stall.

As she stood underneath the warm water, Daniella tried to make sense of her feelings for Brant. Were her emotions real or were her actions toward him based on the fact that she had been in a party mood?

After sorting through her feelings, Daniella decided it didn't make sense to lie to herself any longer about her feelings for Brant. She liked him more than enough. But what if he was just like Ray. Ray was a control freak, Daniella recalled, as she stepped out of the shower and reached for a towel. She dried off and went to her bedroom for her lotion, powder, and perfume. She sat on the edge of her bed, massaging her feet with lotion and remembering the promise that she'd made when she'd divorced Ray.

To start with, she had promised God, herself, and a few other important people that she would never get herself in a messy relationship like that again, Nuh-uh, she mused, getting up off the edge of her bed and going to the closet for her housecoat. But, thinking of all the promises she had made to herself about the affairs of the heart, didn't stop her heart from flipflopping each time she remembered Brant's demanding kisses.

Just as she slipped into her red silk robe, the doorbell rang. Daniella glanced through the blinds and saw her mother's white Cadillac parked in her driveway.

By the time she walked downstairs to open the front door, Daniella had more than one surprise to contend with.

Brant was standing in her living room half-naked,

wearing only his pants, and Annie Mae Taylor stood perched on her three-inch white heels glaring at him. Her silver hair was rolled into a stylish French twist. Annie's jet-black eyes sparked with anger. Her white suit made her appear elegant.

Daniella shifted her eyes from her mother to Brant, allowing her gaze to linger on Brant's bare chest longer than she intended. She turned back to her mother.

"Good morning," Daniella spoke to them both.

"Dannie, I'll explain this later," Brant said, pushing one hand in his pocket, referring to his uninvited sleep over. "Excuse me," he added, taking his shirt from the arm of the sofa, and moving toward the kitchen.

Slowly, Annie Mae switched her glare from Brant's naked chest to Daniella. She propped both hands on her hips.

"When Grace sat on the pew next to me this morning and told me that a man was sleeping in your house, I politely told her it was a sin to lie in church," Annie Mae said to Daniella.

Daniella tightened the sash on her housecoat and walked toward the kitchen. She needed a cup of black coffee before she could begin to think about this matter.

"Dannie, don't you walk away from me when I'm talking to you," Annie Mae's voice rose from its usual low tone.

"Mother, please," Daniella said, taking the mug Brant was holding out to her.

"And don't you 'mother, please' me, child," Annie Mae said, shooting Brant another heated glance.

"Your father will be here in a little while. I'm sure he'll agree with me."

Daniella sipped the coffee before pulling out a stool at the kitchen counter. She sat and turned her attention back to her mother.

"So, is Mrs. Mills my bodyguard?" Daniella asked nonchalantly.

Annie Mae drew in a deep breath and rolled her eyes to the ceiling. "Dannie, I raised you better than this," she said, taking one hand off her hip and patting her hair.

"Mother . . . the last time I looked, I was a grown woman," Daniella said, annoyed that her mother was treating her like a ten-year-old.

"Dannie, I know that. But Grace talks so much, she'll tell all of our friends." Annie Mae glared at Brant again. "And the last thing you need is a ruined reputation."

"Mother . . ." The doorbell rang again interrupting Daniella.

"I'll get it," Brant said, leaving the kitchen and the women alone.

Daniella turned back to her mother. She was glad that Brant was no longer listening to them.

"Mother, I think I'm mature enough to make my own decisions," Daniella said, acknowledging the fact that she hadn't decided where Brant slept last night. Daniella assumed that he had slept in her living room since he wasn't wearing a shirt. She couldn't figure out why he had taken it upon himself to sleep in her living room.

"But Dannie, it'll look a lot better if you married him before he slept in your house," Annie Mae replied.

Daniella slid off the stool and went to the refrigerator and pushed the ice button. She dropped a cube in her coffee and threw the extra ice in the sink. The next time Brant slept in her house, she at least wanted to know about it.

"Mother, I'm not interested in marriage," Daniella said.

"Just because you got yourself tangled up with that disgusting, good-for-nothing, poor excuse for a man the first time, doesn't mean you can't get married again, Dannie," Annie Mae said. "Ray's probably in Florida right now making some woman miserable."

"Ray's dead, Mother," Daniella said and took another sip of coffee.

Annie Mae looked as if she had been slapped in the face. "Oh my God, please forgive me for speaking ill of the dead."

Daniella's father, Jake, and Brant walked into the kitchen.

Jake stood in the doorway, while Brant leaned comfortably against the doorjamb, with his hands planted on his hips.

Jake cleared his throat.

"How are you, Dannie?" her father asked, interrupting Daniella and Annie Mae's discussion.

If it weren't for his silver hair, mustache, and short, neat beard, Jake would've looked every bit of sixty, instead of his seventy years.

"Daddy," Daniella said, smiling, going over to give her father a hug. "The islands agreed with you," she said, standing back admiring him.

Annie Mae waved her manicured hands toward the ceiling. "You didn't compliment me," Annie Mae said to Daniella.

"You didn't give me a chance," Daniella replied. "But you look lovely."

Annie Mae smiled. "Thank you, darling." She turned to Brant. "Young man, under the circumstances, it was nice to meet you."

Brant nodded.

"Annie Mae, I think it's time for us to leave," Jake said, going over and taking his wife's hand.

"Yes, I think so," she said, planting a kiss on Daniella's cheek.

"Brant take it easy." Jake shook Brant's hand.

"Same here, sir," Brant said.

Annie Mae looked at Daniella and smiled. "Honey, I just want to see you happy," she said to Daniella as if Brant was a threat to her only child.

Annie Mae turned back to Brant.

Daniella walked out to the car with her parents. Two minutes later, she was inside her kitchen.

Brant chuckled. "Your mother is a tough woman, babe."

Daniella stood before Brant with her hands planted firmly on her hips.

"Why didn't you tell me that you were sleeping here last night?" Daniella said.

"Are you in trouble?" Brant leaned against the counter and gazed at Daniella.

"Trouble . . . what're you talking about?" Daniella asked Brant as if she weren't aware of the phone calls that had started a few days ago. Brant wouldn't know that. Had he been talking to Jerry? If so, she planned to remind Jerry not to discuss her problems with Brant.

"Someone called you last night and threatened

you, Dannie. I didn't think it was safe to leave you alone," Brant replied.

Black fear coiled in Daniella's stomach. She had been half-asleep last night when Brant drove her home. She'd forgotten to turn the ringer on the kitchen phone off.

"It's just some nut making crank calls," Daniella said, sounding braver than she felt.

Brant reached out and drew Daniella to him. "If you say so. But I think you need to buy a Caller ID or get your number changed. As Brant spoke, he seemed to be searching Daniella's eyes for signs of fear.

"I'll be all right," Daniella assured him, snuggling close to Brant. To her, Brant's embrace was a protective shield from Ray's mean friends.

"I don't want anything to happen to you, Dannie," Brant told her, lowering his head, pausing as if he was giving Daniella a chance to pull away. He brushed his lips against her cheek, his mustache tickling her skin. His lips moved to hers and he kissed her lightly.

"I have to go home," he said, giving her another light kiss. "I'll see you later."

Daniella felt the familiar heart fluttering that she always experienced when she was near Brant. A shiver ran over her, and she closed her eyes. *You should tell Brant about your problem,* a small voice in the back of Daniella's mind whispered. She ignored the warning. Why should she burden Brant with her problem? It wouldn't be long before Jerry found Ray's friend and handed him over to the police.

Slowly, Daniella untangled herself from Brant's embrace, and walked him to the door. Later, she was going to Beverly's son's birthday party. Daniella

glanced at the clock. She hadn't bought T.J. a birthday gift. She ran upstairs and changed into a blue
shorts set, stuck her feet into a pair of black thongs,
and grabbed her purse on her way out of her bedroom.

Three miles later, Daniella parked in front of the
toy store. Children of all ages stood in the aisles of
the store, playing with games and toys. It had been
years since Daniella had gone into a toy store. She
avoided the place like the plague most times. Toy
stores usually reminded her of the children she
wanted, but was too afraid to have without a husband.
And she wasn't about to get married again, so having
children was out.

Daniella chose the 1-2-3 bike for T.J.'s birthday gift,
thinking how T.J. would enjoy riding on the red, blue,
and yellow toy. She had moved back to get a better
look at the price, when she felt someone behind her.

"Excuse me," Daniella said.

"I think the bike is a good choice," Brant said,
moving around to stand next to Daniella.

Daniella glanced at Brant, his face seemed smooth
from shaving. She allowed her gaze to slide over the
rest of him, observing that he had changed into a
pair of jeans and a gray sleeveless pullover. Slowly,
she shifted her gaze to his mouth, as the subtle scent
of his rich cologne floated over her.

"What're you doing here?" Daniella asked, surprised to see Brant twice that day.

"I remembered I hadn't bought T.J. a birthday
gift," Brant said, grinning.

"I forgot too," Daniella said, taking another look
at the price on the 1-2-3 bike box.

"Yeah, that usually happens when you don't have

kids," Brant said, taking a box of beginner's inline skates for children from a lower shelf.

"I would love to buy him another toy, but I'm afraid Beverly will half kill me if I do." Daniella chuckled.

"Don't you think we have enough toys for T.J. to play with?" Brant asked Daniella, putting the inline skates in a shopping cart, then setting the 1-2-3 bike next to the skates.

"I think these gifts will keep T.J. satisfied for a little while," Daniella said, laughing, as she and Brant walked to the checkout counter like a husband and wife who had just finished shopping for their child's Christmas gifts.

Brant took Daniella's gift from the shopping cart and set it on the checkout counter.

"I'll pay," he said, reaching in his pocket for his wallet.

Daniella turned around and gazed at Brant. "Keep your money," she said in a low voice so that the other customers wouldn't hear her.

"But, I want to," Brant said.

Daniella just stared at him.

"All right—all right," Brant said, taking enough money from his wallet to pay for his purchase.

After they paid for their gifts, Brant and Daniella pushed the cart out to her Jeep. They walked slowly across the parking lot like an old married couple.

"I got it," Brant said, taking the bike out of the cart after Daniella had unlocked the tailgate to her Jeep.

Daniella smiled to herself. Brant wanted to do everything for her except give her back the job she loved doing.

"I'll see you later," Daniella said, climbing into the

Jeep 4x4. She tried not to look at him as he trotted across the parking lot to his truck. *Lord, that man is fine,* Daniella told herself as she climbed into her Jeep. *What am I going to do about this? Nothing, not a darn thing,* she decided. *I'll go with the flow. If nothing but a little fun comes out of this relationship with Brant, I deserve it. Why not enjoy myself? Brant Parker can't hurt me unless I let him,* Daniella thought as she drove the six miles to T.J.'s birthday party.

Daniella pulled up beside Beverly's Lexus in front of her and Tyrone's ranch home. She could hear the children laughing and squealing from the backyard as she neared the back gate. Daniella lifted the latch and walked around the house to the backyard. Beverly and Tyrone had strung colorful balloons across the yard, on tree trunks, and every tree limb and twig that was available.

When Daniella walked into the backyard, Beverly had just finished covering the birthday table with paper that had the animated drawings of all of T.J.'s favorite cartoon characters on it.

"Hey girl," Beverly said, walking up to Daniella.

"Hi," Daniella said, setting the box down next to the other gifts near a tree by the back gate.

"How was your dinner party?" Beverly asked.

Daniella pressed her lips together, smothering a smile.

"A disaster. So we went to The Glow."

"That's the Dannie I know," Beverly said.

"Which doesn't mean that I'm letting you off the hook for not coming," Daniella said.

"I swear Dannie, if Tyrone's half-brother wasn't here, Tyrone and I would've been there," Beverly said, pointing to the edge of her patio, where Tyrone's half-brother and his wife were talking to some employees from Parker's Art.

The couple were dressed in denim shorts and T-shirts. Tyrone's half-brother didn't resemble Tyrone. He was short and heavy and about an inch taller than his wife.

"They look happy," Daniella said.

"I guess they are, girl," Beverly said. "But I want to know what happened between you and Brant last night to make you change your mind," Beverly said.

"A lot happened. But I think I'll take one day at a time," Daniella said, just as T.J. slid around the corner of the patio.

"Aunt Dannie . . . hi," T.J. said, half-jumping and half-skipping up to Daniella with outstretched arms.

Daniella squatted and held out her arms to hug her godchild.

"Hey little man," Daniella said, wrapping her arms around T.J.'s little waist. "Are you having fun?"

"Yes," T.J. said, giving Daniella a tight hug. "The clown is inside," T.J. said to Daniella.

"Ooh, really?" Daniella said, smiling at T.J. "I love clowns."

"I'll go get her," T.J. said, wheeling himself out of Daniella's arms. "Hey clown, come here!" T.J. yelled, running inside the house. It wasn't long before little T.J. ran out of the house laughing and holding his stomach, with the clown smack-dab on his heels. He ran to his mother, folding his arms around Beverly's bare legs.

"See?" he said, pointing to the short female clown and laughing.

Daniella couldn't help but laugh. The clown was dressed in big, red, baggy pants and a yellow shirt with short, puffy sleeves. She wore long red and yellow shoes, a red curly wig, and smiling red lips that covered half her face.

The clown bowed before Daniella, cut a dance step, and skipped off to play with the other children.

T.J. rolled on the grass, laughing. "Isn't she cool, Aunt Dannie?" T.J. asked pointing to the frisky clown.

"Yes, she is," Daniella said, laughing. She gave T.J.'s cheeks a playful pinch.

T.J. grinned, and ran off to join his friends.

Daniella and Beverly headed toward the patio to join the others and take T.J.'s gift inside. While crossing the lawn, Beverly turned to Daniella.

"You know, Dannie, I'm glad that you've made up your mind to get on with your life."

Uncertain of the decision she had made to date Brant, Daniella smiled. "I figured it this way, I don't have a thing to lose," she replied as they reached the patio.

A few of the staff members from Parker's Art were sitting around the patio table. Joyce, Karen, and their husbands had been invited to bring their children to T.J.'s birthday party.

"Hi," Daniella spoke, looking around for a chair.

The adults spoke to Daniella in unison, interrupting their conversation on marriage.

"Marriage is a business. It's as simple as that," Joyce said. Her lemon complexion glowed as she shared her experienced views on marital issues. She crossed her long legs and let Karen, who had raised her hand, talk.

"Of course it is. But let's remember, Joyce, marriage can also be good. Like everything else, it's what you make it," Karen said, looking out in the yard where the men and Tyrone were talking. She got her husband's attention and gave him a seductive smile.

"True," Joyce said, then glanced at Daniella and grinned. "Let's talk about something else. We have single people here, Karen." Joyce smiled at Daniella.

"Don't stop on my account," Daniella said, acting as if she hadn't noticed Joyce's effort to smooth things over. She'd once thought the sentiments of matrimony were all flowers and chocolates. Of course, she knew better now. If and when she ever made up her mind to leap into another so-called wedded bliss, she, too, would know what to look for.

Daniella cast a brief glance out in the backyard and noticed that Brant had arrived. He and Tyrone had their heads together and seemed to be engaged in an intense conversation.

Daniella leaned back in her chair and closed her eyes, as if doing so would shut out the conversation on love and marriage. She understood all too well the tangled web of marriage, and she couldn't call it a business.

Obviously Ray hadn't understood the meaning of the nuptial knot. When she realized that he was greedy, selfish, and controlling, Daniella asked him for a divorce. Ray refused, saying that he didn't believe in divorce. According to his wedding vows, Ray was married until death did them part. And besides, Ray informed Daniella that she had no grounds to divorce him—she was just upset because she couldn't have her way.

Determined to free herself from a man possessed with greed and control, Daniella called Jerry and had him search for anything he could find on Ray. She was certain that Ray had some skeletons in his closet since he didn't come home from work until midnight most nights, if he came home at all.

What Jerry found out about Ray sent Daniella into a tailspin, making her wish that she had never known Ray Spencer.

The children's giggles drew Daniella out of her retrospections of her spoiled marriage. She sat quietly watching the clown end a game of Duck, Duck, Goose with the children.

"I won, I won!" Karen's little girl said, skipping to her mother. "I get the prize," she said.

"You did not," T.J. said, running behind the little girl. "I won."

"You didn't, T.J." Joyce's son ran to the patio, defending his little friend. "Just ask the clown."

"No," T.J. said, running out on the lawn, falling down, kicking, and beating his small fists against the grass.

"Hey . . . hey, T.J." Tyrone turned away from Brant and went to his son. "What's wrong with you, man?"

"I want to win. It's my party," Daniella heard T.J. say. She didn't hear anymore of the father-and-son conversation. Brant was moving toward her, grinning.

"What's up," Brant said, when he reached Daniella. He sat on the rail of the patio and looked at her.

"I'm just watching these kids," Daniella said, smiling, noticing that T.J. and the other children had calmed down and were playing another game.

"Red light," Daniella heard the clown say to the children. Daniella and Brant chuckled as they sat watching the children ease across the lawn behind the clown.

"Dannie, Karen, Joyce. I need some help in here." Daniella heard Beverly call from the kitchen.

Daniella, Karen, and Joyce left the other guests and went inside, helping Beverly carry out the birthday hats, food, cake, and ice cream. They set the food on the table. Brant and the other guys helped the children wash their hands at the outside faucet, then seated the children at the table.

When Brant finished helping with the children, he walked over and stood beside Daniella.

"I want at least two children. What about you?" Brant asked Daniella.

Daniella's face broke into a smile. It never occurred to her that Brant wanted children. Then her smile faded as she remembered how she had tried to get pregnant when she was with Ray. She hadn't been able to have a child. The doctor told her she was too stressed out.

"I would like a couple of kids myself," Daniella stated, glancing at Brant. *But I'm not brave enough to get married again,* she thought.

"We can do that, you know," Brant said, chuckling under his breath.

"We?" Daniella smothered a smile.

"Yeah," Brant said.

Daniella glanced out at the children biting into mini burgers, eating French fries, and drinking milk shakes from small paper cups. Brant's teasing was not funny. Marriage and children were serious business.

Finally, the children finished eating. The clown slipped the sing-along happy birthday disc into the portable stereo and the children and adults sang happy birthday to T.J.

When the singing ended, T.J. stood up in his chair while Beverly lit the three blue candles on the white sheet cake that was decorated with a baseball and bat and letters that read, Happy Birthday T.J.

"Blow hard, T.J." Tyrone said as T.J. filled his cheeks with air and began blowing the candles out.

"Yeahhhh!" The crowd screamed, clapping their hands after T.J. blew out the candles.

After the cake was cut and served and the gifts were opened, Joyce's son decided he wanted to take the light blue ball with white stars home with him.

"Mommy, why can't I take my ball home with me?" Kareem asked, his eyes welling with tears.

"Because you gave it to T.J. for his birthday, honey," Joyce said, trying to make Kareem understand that he couldn't take the ball he had given T.J. home with him.

"But it's mine," Kareem cried.

"Lord have mercy, boy. Beverly, I'll see you at work tomorrow. I'm taking this child home and put him to bed," Joyce said.

When all the guests had left the birthday party, and Beverly had bathed and put T.J. to bed, Daniella and Brant helped Tyrone and Beverly clean up. When they finished, Daniella dropped down in a nearby chair. Brant sank down beside her.

"Man, those kids have plenty of energy," Brant said, giving Daniella a side glance.

"It wore me out just looking at them," Daniella said, returning Brant's glance. "Have you changed your mind about wanting children?" she asked.

"No."

Daniella laughed.

Beverly came over to where Daniella and Brant were sitting and leaned against the patio rail.

"T.J. is in bed. We might as well play a game of

Spades," Beverly suggested, switching her gaze from Daniella to Brant.

"Might as well," Brant said, getting up to help Tyrone set up the card table.

"Did you pack for your trip to Georgia?" Beverly asked Daniella as soon as Brant was out of hearing distance.

"Bev, it's not like I'm going to Atlanta. All I need to pack are some shorts, jeans, and shirts," Daniella remarked.

"I don't know, Dannie. Tyrone and I went to a small town in Georgia and we went to a nice club," Beverly said.

"Believe me, Bev, where we're going, I don't think there is a club," Daniella said. "Anyway, I'm not going to have time to pack very much, since I'm working late next week," Daniella added.

"I'm leaving work early Friday, if you don't mind, I can pack your luggage," Beverly offered.

"Really, Beverly?" Daniella asked.

"Sure," Beverly said, glancing at the kitchen door. Tyrone and Brant came out on the patio.

"I'd appreciate it because I do have to get my hair done," Daniella said, as Brant and Tyrone dragged back chairs and sat at the card table.

"That's right, sit down, so Beverly and I can beat the pants off you," Daniella said.

"Dannie, babe, you can beat the pants off me anytime you want." Brant chuckled.

"You got that right," Tyrone said, reaching for the cards. "Right, Beverly?"

"Ah, shut up, that's all you guys think about," Beverly said, glancing at Tyrone.

The warm sound of Brant's laughter made Daniella's heart flutter, as she remembered his gentle kisses that had made her change her mind about dating again.

"All right, we'll play, but. . .we're playing for stakes," Tyrone said, drawing Daniella back to the present.

"Uh uh, we're not playing for money," Daniella said.

"I heard that," Beverly said.

"Ah, come on, babe, let's make the game fun," Tyrone pleaded with his wife.

"All right," Brant snapped his fingers, and said to Tyrone. "If Dannie and Beverly win, we'll take them on a weekend trip anywhere they want to go," Brant said. "And if they lose, we'll settle for a night out on the town."

"Sounds like a plan to me," Tyrone agreed with his partner.

Daniella smiled. "Well, I want to go to the Bahamas."

"Don't worry, you're not going because we're winning this game," Brant said.

Tyrone grinned.

Daniella stole a glance at Brant. *He's mighty sure of himself,* she thought, hoping that she and Beverly would win the card game. If she won, she wasn't sure if she could handle a weekend with Brant on the white sandy beaches in the Bahamas.

"All right, these are the rules," Tyrone said. "No cheating, no talking over the table, no touching toes, and . . ."

"And you can talk," Daniella said to Tyrone. "If I catch you and Brant looking at each other, this game is over." Daniella took the cards from Tyrone and started shuffling. "Because Beverly and I are winning," Daniella said, fanning the deck.

"You got that right, Dannie. That trip to anywhere we want to go sounds good to me," Beverly said.

"Ummm hmmm," Daniella said, sliding the deck to Brant for him to cut.

Daniella, Brant, and Tyrone played Spades until around ten that Sunday night. When the game was over, Brant grinned at Daniella.

"All right, Dannie, when do you want to go to the Bahamas?" Brant asked.

"I'll let you know," Daniella answered, lowering her eyes to avoid Brant's seductive gaze.

"Don't take too long making up your mind, I have to make reservations," Brant replied, getting up from the table, stretching.

"I'll let you know in plenty of time," Daniella said, getting up, folding her chair, and leaning it against the patio's rail and walking to her Jeep as she said goodnight to Beverly and Tyrone. She felt her face warm. She didn't know if she remembered how to act on a weekend trip with a man. It had been a long time since she'd done anything like that.

"I'll see you tomorrow," Daniella said when Brant caught up with her and slipped his arms around her waist.

"I'll call you," he said, walking her to her Jeep. Before he took the key from her hand, he leaned over and gave her a light kiss on her lips.

"Are you going to be all right tonight?" Brant asked Daniella, referring to the phone calls she had been receiving.

"Sure, I'll be fine," Daniella said. Reminding herself to turn off all the phone ringers.

"Don't forget to get the Caller ID," Brant reminded her.

"I'll buy one next week," Daniella said, inhaling the scent of Brant's cologne.

He lowered his head once more and touched her lips with his.

The soft touch of Brant's lips against hers, sent shivers through her. She climbed in her Jeep, and silently prayed that she hadn't gotten herself into a situation that she would later regret.

"See you," Daniella said to Brant, blowing him a kiss.

CHAPTER 10

Early Friday morning, Brant dragged his luggage out of his bedroom closet and started packing: faded blue jeans, T-shirts, sneakers, dress shoes, blue suit.

When Brant first told Daniella that they were going to Georgia to work on the project, he never assumed that Cupid would've shot an arrow, making his and Daniella's relationship more than boss and employee.

Brant finished packing, got dressed, and threw his luggage in the back of his pickup and drove to work.

Daniella had told him yesterday that she would meet him at Newark International Airport. She had a few chores to do before she left New Jersey, Brant recalled Daniella saying as he drove to Parker's Art.

Sprinting on the edge of that recollection came the thought of how perfect Daniella would fit into his life.

She was just the type of woman that would make

a good wife for him and mother for his children. He'd noticed how attentive she had been toward T.J. *Cool it, Brant, just because the woman is showing you some affection, doesn't mean that she's ready to become Mrs. Brant Parker,* Brant thought as he stopped at the traffic light.

The traffic light changed to green and Brant pressed the gas pedal, accelerating much too fast for the speed limit. He glanced down at the speedometer and slowed down. It had gotten to the point where he could hardly wait to see Daniella every day. She would probably be wearing one of those flare-tail dresses or a pair of jeans, Brant reflected. It didn't matter what she wore, Miss Daniella Taylor looked good in anything she put on.

At that moment, Brant wished that Daniella was beside him. He wanted to touch her, to smell her sweet scent, to taste and feel her lips against his. Easy, easy, easy, Brant thought. He had made some headway in the romance department with Daniella, but still, he didn't want to rush her. He understood that she'd had a problem with her marriage. He had to make her understand that he was not like her ex-husband. From now on, Brant decided to let the sweet Miss Taylor make all the first moves.

Brant pulled up to another traffic light. While he waited for the signal to change, for some reason he reflected on his past life. Like when he was a young boy, he had a speech problem. For years, he had stuttered. His parents had taken him to a speech therapist and by the time he was in his teens, his speech problem had almost disappeared. The only time he stuttered now was when he was excited, nervous, or very angry.

Brant wasn't sure what had been the reason for his

speech problem. When he was a kid, he was shy, although, his parents didn't treat him and his older brother Nick any different. They sent them to the best schools, and could afford to let them travel every other summer to a foreign country when they were in their teens.

Brant liked Africa all right. He'd made a couple of friends, but the food was too hot and spicy for his taste.

He adored Paris. Maybe it was because he discovered his love for romance. He was popular with the ladies, which had a lot to do with his improved self-esteem.

However, being shy had never been a problem for Nick. Nick seemed to love debating a subject, even when he was a boy. Brant remembered when Nick announced to the family over dinner that he wanted to become a lawyer. Brant's parents had been disappointed that Nick was only interested in attending to legal issues of Parker's Art, but in the end Mark and Clara had agreed not to stand in the way of their son's career choice.

While Nick read every book in the library on law, Brant had sketched pictures from memory, and in his imagination, built model homes and buildings and followed his dad around Parker's Art every chance he got. His parents were proud of his talents and his potential to operate Parker's Art. So they sent Brant to architectural school.

However, because of Brant's popularity with the women, he acquired an overblown ego, which caused a problem for him while in college. As a result of his philandering, Brant graduated a year late from college. For Brant's punishment, his father hired him to work as a carpenter, instead of a draftsperson and a designer, when he finally graduated.

Brant had to work long, hard hours in the summer and winter. He had hated every minute of it, especially when the grouchy head carpenter assigned him a job that he disliked, like the time he ordered Brant to work on the roof. Brant had lost his balance and fell, breaking his leg. While Brant recuperated from his injury, he promised himself that if he was ever promoted from carpenter to architect, he would follow his father's rules to the letter, which included the rule of not dating Parker's Art employees.

When Daniella was hired to work for his father's company, Brant began to have a change of heart, until his daddy pulled his coattail reminding him of the company's policy. As it turned out, Brant had watched Daniella resign her interior design position and get married. But fate had given him another chance with Daniella. He was the head man in charge at Parker's Art now and the no-dating-employee policy was rescinded.

Brant parked in front of Parker's Art, got out of his pickup, and half-jogged into the building.

"Good morning," he said to the receptionist on his way to his office.

"Good morning," the middle-aged woman said, giving Brant a surprised glance. Probably because he was never cheerful early in the morning.

"Morning, Joyce," Brant said, thumping on Joyce's open office door.

"Hey, why're you so happy this morning?" Joyce looked up from her work.

Brant grinned, shrugged, and headed down to

Tyrone's work area. He thumped on the door and went inside before Tyrone could invite him in.

"What's going on, man?" Brant said, sliding into a chair, facing Tyrone.

"I don't know, but you look like you just won the lottery," Tyrone chuckled.

Brant leaned back, locked his hands behind his head, and winked. "I feel like it," he said.

"Oh . . . you and Dannie are going to Georgia. Now I understand." Tyrone chuckled.

Brant unlocked his hands from behind his head and rubbed his hands over his face. "Tyrone, I'm excited," Brant said, still grinning.

Tyrone threw his head back, roaring with peals of laughter. "Come on, guy, I know you're not . . . what is the word I'm looking for." Tyrone frowned. "Yeah, jittery." Tyrone held out his hands, making them tremble as if he were nervous.

Brant gave his buddy a deadpan gaze. "When—ah-you fell—" Brant stopped, took a couple of deep breaths, and continued, "in love with Beverly, did I make fun of you?"

Tyrone straightened in his chair. "No, but I've never seen you this anxious about a woman before."

Brant stood and crossed the room. He pushed his hands in his pockets. "I can't do anything to mess this up, Tyrone."

"Like what?" Tyrone asked, more serious this time.

"I don't know. I'm not sure that Daniella wants me," Brant stated.

"Tck, tck, tck, Brant you're doubting yourself," Tyrone rubbed his finger over his mustache, hiding a grin with his palm.

"Okay, go ahead and laugh, Tyrone," Brant said, turning to leave.

"I'm trying to be helpful here," Tyrone teased.

"Ah—Tyrone shut up," Brant said, walking out of his buddy's office. Brant stopped. "I've employed two more college students to work on the Gains project. You can expect them in your office at nine-thirty tomorrow morning," Brant informed Tyrone.

College students were often sent to Parker's Art from the community center or the Urban League to volunteer their services in the architectural field. Brant had hired the students paying them a little more than minimum wage. Most of the students were poor and struggling and could use the money.

"Good," Tyrone said, "I'll be expecting them."

Brant gave Tyrone the telephone number where he could be reached in Georgia. "I'll see you later."

"Take it easy, man, and have a safe trip and a good time," Tyrone said, just as Brant reached the door.

Brant shot Tyrone a cool glance over his shoulder, walked out, and slammed the door. As thick as the walls were, he could hear Tyrone laughing.

The lights were off in Brant's and Daniella's office. Usually when the room was dark, it meant that Daniella hadn't arrived. Brant glanced around the room before opening the blinds. He recognized Daniella's black briefcase sitting on the work counter.

He didn't have to wonder where Daniella was. It was clear she was in the interior design department. Brant felt sort of guilty for assigning Daniella to work with him.

He knew Daniella loved her work. But it was something that couldn't be helped. He had a business to run, and whether Daniella liked it or not wasn't a problem for him.

Besides, Parker's Art's expertise was redesigning old residences, upgrading the homes, making them look new again, Brant considered. His father had included the interior design department because he had gotten lots of requests for decorative projects once the houses were completed.

If it were left up to Brant, he would not have opened an interior design department in the first place. *But then you would've never met the lovely Miss Taylor,* a small voice in the back of his mind reminded him.

Brant groaned. All of a sudden, a terrifying thought crossed his mind. Suppose Daniella was pretending to want him as much as he wanted her just so she could get her old job back. Brant rested one hand on his narrow hip. *By the time I get through loving Miss Taylor, beautifying a house will be the last thing on her mind.*

CHAPTER 11

The beauty salon was quiet except for the soft whine of several blow-dryers. Daniella sank down in Zelda's styling chair and glanced over at several women sitting underneath hair dryers with multicolored rollers in their hair. Next to the ladies, a man sat under a dryer reading the day's *Star-Ledger*. For a moment, Daniella stared at him. She wondered if he was her stalker. She shifted in her chair, straining to get a better look at him. His skin was dark, and he wore black horn-rimmed glasses. It looked as if he had a few dozen of Zelda's blue perm rods in his hair. The man didn't look like any of Ray's friends to Daniella. However, she hadn't met all of Ray's friends in the four years that they were married.

Daniella dismissed her fears. She checked her watch, crossed one leg over the other, and swung her foot to the beat of a tune playing on the radio. There was no way she was going to make it to Newark International in time to make the flight to Georgia with Brant.

Daniella knew that Zelda was slow, so she'd called and asked the beautician if she could come an hour early. Of course Zelda had told Daniella that she could accept her. After all, Daniella had been going to Zelda's since she was a senior in high school. Nevertheless, Zelda hadn't sped up much when it came to styling hair.

Daniella gave her watch another impatient glance. *Brant is going to kill me,* she thought, letting out a long sigh and waiting for Zelda to start blow-drying her hair.

"Dannie, I don't know what you're sitting up here breathing loud for. You know it has always taken me a long time to do your hair," Zelda reminded her.

"I know, Zelda," Daniella agreed. But she had promised Brant that she would meet him at the airport. Daniella took out her cellular phone and dialed Brant's number. Of all the times for him to have his phone off, Daniella thought, dialing the number to Newark International Airport. If she couldn't get another flight out tonight, she was in big trouble. Here she was worrying over losing her interior design job. If she didn't make it to Georgia on time, she would be lucky to have a job at all, Daniella thought, waiting for an airline agent to answer her phone call.

Luckily, the reservation's clerk told Daniella that they'd had a few cancellations. Daniella could take the nine o'clock flight to Atlanta.

Satisfied with the flight arrangements, Daniella relaxed and allowed sensual thoughts of Brant to play around the edges of her mind.

First of all, what were they going to do after their work was done? Or as far as that mattered, what would they do in between work hours. Daniella felt her heart flutter. Would Brant kiss her again? Or would he be all business? All week she and Brant had been busy. They hadn't talked much to each other, and when they did, it was usually to discuss their work in Georgia. Daniella had begun to wonder if Brant had changed his mind about his feelings for her. *It doesn't matter,* Daniella decided. *I don't have time for romance anyway.* But, it would be nice, she thought, catching a glimpse of herself in Zelda's styling mirror. She didn't realize that she was smiling.

"It must be nice," Zelda commented.

"What?" Daniella asked.

"Usually when my clients are smiling, the love is good," Zelda laughed.

"What?" Daniella widened her eyes, as if she didn't know what Zelda was referring to.

"Don't try to play it off. Grace Mills was in here the other day, and honey, she told me all about that new man you have in your life," Zelda said.

"I don't know what I'm going to do about that woman," Daniella said, chuckling.

"Don't pay her no mind, she's just old, nosy, and don't have anything else to do," Zelda said.

Daniella smiled, shaking her head slowly. "I guess you have a point," she said, dialing Jerry's PI service to give him her Georgia phone number, just in case he found more information on the man who was stalking and threatening her.

"Jerry, I'll be in Georgia this weekend. If you come across anything I need to know, give me a call," Daniella said, while Zelda stood behind her winding strands of her hair on the marcel iron.

"I might be on to something, Dannie. I'm glad you called," Jerry said.

"Really. What?" Daniella asked, glancing at the man who was still sitting in the dryer's chair.

"Like I said, Dannie, I'm not sure. But this guy knows every move you make," Jerry said.

Daniella cast a quick glance at the dark-skinned man sitting across from her. He grinned, flashing a gold tooth.

"Oh my God," Daniella whispered in the receiver to Jerry.

"What's going on, Dannie?" Jerry asked.

"A man is sitting in Zelda's beauty salon," Daniella said. "And he's watching me."

"All right, I'll see you in a few minutes," Jerry said.

"Jerry it's not necessary. . ."

The phone went dead. For a moment, Daniella just stared at the hard, black plastic, before slipping it back in her purse. Why Ray's hoodlum friends thought she had money to pay for Ray's debt was beyond her. It was just like Ray. He was dead as a hammer. But being the phantom he was, Ray still found ways to harass her.

Daniella pulled out the money from her purse and paid and tipped Zelda.

"Have a good time, Dannie," Zelda said, smiling.

"I'm going to work, not to party," Daniella said, realizing that Zelda had overheard her phone conversation.

"Have a good time anyway." Zelda laughed.

"If I find any amusement in those woods, I'll let you know when I get back," Daniella said, checking to see if the man at the dryer was still watching her. The seat he had been sitting in was empty. Daniella figured he was at the shampoo bowl with Zelda's assistant.

Daniella turned her attention to her reflection in the mirror. Her hair flowed around her shoulders, bouncy and healthy. It was a pity that she was going to the Georgia woods and no one was going to see what an excellent job Zelda had done. With that depressing thought in mind, Daniella waited in the reception area for Jerry.

True to his promise, Jerry walked into the salon, not long after Daniella had seated herself.

"Where is he?" Jerry asked Daniella.

"I think he's at the shampoo bowl," Daniella whispered to keep from being heard by the other patrons.

Jerry stepped to the front of the receptionist's desk and leaned back to get a better look at the shampoo area in the back of the salon.

"I can't see him," Jerry said. "His head is too far back in the shampoo bowl." Jerry walked over to Daniella, "Which one of these women is Zelda?" Jerry asked Daniella.

Daniella nodded in the direction of her beautician. Jerry walked over to Zelda. "Excuse me. Can I use your rest room?" Daniella heard Jerry ask. Zelda nodded, pointing to the small rest room in the back of the shop. Daniella watched as Jerry walked slowly, stopping and lingering a few moments in front of the man at the shampoo bowl.

In about two minutes, Jerry was back.

"He's not the guy I'm looking for," Jerry told Daniella.

Daniella was relieved that the man hadn't been her stalker.

"Thanks, Jerry," Daniella said, getting up to go to her Jeep.

"Dannie, for your protection, I'll drive you to the airport," Jerry said.

"Jerry, I'll be fine," Daniella said, "I have my Mace." She patted the black tube hooked to her key chain.

"I insist," Jerry said, walking Daniella to her Jeep.

"Okay."

At exactly ten o'clock, Daniella's flight touched down at Atlanta's airport. She hurried off the plane and through the crowd to collect her bags and then went to the rental car station. While she waited for the paperwork on the car, Daniella called Brant.

After the first ring, Brant answered the phone.

"Hello," Daniella said, and waited for Brant to return her greeting.

"Where are you?" Brant asked her. His voice sounded tired.

Daniella crossed one ankle over the other and propped her elbow on the counter. "I'm in Atlanta. I'm renting a car. Did I answer all of your questions?" Daniella requested in a firm tone.

"No," Brant said. "Don't rent the car, I'm coming to get you."

"But—" Daniella started to tell Brant that if he gave her the directions, she would be at the house in an hour or two. But before she could argue with him, Brant had slammed the phone down. She jumped from the sound of the receiver crashing against the phone's cradle.

"I'm sorry," Daniella said to the rental car agent. "I won't need the car after all."

An hour and a half later, Brant stormed into the Hertz car rental office. His eyes were red from exhaustion, Daniella suspected. But she was certain that the hard lines around his mouth were a sign of how angry at her he really was.

"Where is your luggage?" Brant asked, glancing at her.

Daniella nodded in the direction of her luggage. First of all, angry or not, Daniella didn't like Brant's attitude one bit.

"You didn't have to come here for me," Daniella said, glaring at Brant, as they headed out to his rented truck.

"I guess you know where you're going," Brant shot back.

"I had planned to use a map," Daniella said, waiting for Brant to unlock the truck's door on the passenger's side. When he reached around her to stick the key in the lock, Daniella heard him chuckle under his breath.

"I'm not afraid to travel alone," Daniella said, remembering when she had driven from Virginia to New Jersey while she was in college. Her parents had a conniption fit. However, their worries were useless. Daniella had dressed like a man, and she had sat one of those dummy men in the passenger's seat so it wouldn't look like she was traveling alone.

"I didn't say you couldn't, but I'll guarantee you, a map won't do you any good out here tonight."

Daniella glared at him.

"Are you going to stand there all night, or are we going home?" Brant asked, slipping his hands around her waist, lifting her onto the truck's seat.

"I think I should drive. You look tired," Daniella said, sliding across the seat to the driver's side.

"Are you sure?" Brant inquired, gazing at Daniella.

"Give me the directions," Daniella said.

Brant got in. "All right. You're going to drive about sixty miles before you come to a small town. You'll come to an intersection. There's a police station on the left and a restaurant on the right side of the street. Make sure you stop at the caution light. We don't want to get a traffic ticket," Brant instructed.

Daniella glanced at Brant and smiled while he continued to give her instructions.

"Don't turn off the main highway because about four or five miles down the road, you'll see a large, white house from the top of the hill. Start slowing down, and get ready to turn off onto a lane," he said, leaning back against the seat. "That's the house we'll be living in this weekend."

"Okay," Daniella said, starting the truck's engine. Before she could drive out of the rental car office's parking lot, Brant was asleep. Daniella turned on the radio and listened to the sound of a country singer's sad lyrics about losing her "Sweet Thing." A surge of sensuality washed over Daniella as she cherished the kisses she and Brant had shared the night of her ruined dinner party. But tonight, he hadn't attempted to kiss her. Daniella glanced at him beside her. Brant had scooted down in the seat, his hands were lying between his thighs, his head resting comfortably on the headrest.

One hour later, Daniella slowed and stopped at the

yellow flashing caution light at the four-way intersection. Sure enough, the restaurant and police station
were positioned as Brant had said. However, he
hadn't mention the row of white houses that sat along
the narrow highway. Daniella glanced at the clock on
the dash panel. It was after midnight. She drove
slower after reading the warning sign to watch out for
deer crossing the road. Besides, the fog had thickened
and it was hard to see. Four miles after she passed
the intersection, Daniella turned onto the lane. The
big, white house sat on the hill. Through the darkness,
she saw a tall aqua streetlight standing in the yard.
The only other light was a dim lamplight shining
through the wide picture window of the two-story
house that rose over a thick green, manicured lawn.
Two Georgia pines stood on the left and right of the
house.

Daniella reached out and touched Brant's broad
shoulders, shaking him lightly.

"Wake up Brant," she said, giving him another
light shake.

"Hmmm—all right," Brant groaned, getting out
of the truck, stretching before he took Daniella's luggage off the back.

They climbed the steel-blue steps to the porch.

"Which key opens the door?" Daniella asked, turning the keys on the key ring over in her hand.

"The door is open," Brant said.

"Now I know I'm in the backwoods. No one in
their right mind leaves the door to a house open,"
Daniella said, turning the doorknob, walking into the
wide foyer.

"This is the country, Dannie," Brant said, walking
up the winding stairs, carrying her luggage.

"You could've fool me." Daniella smothered a smile, and checked out her new surroundings.

A glass table sat against the wall. In the center of the table was a crystal vase filled with a dozen red roses. Two cushioned chairs the color of pink salmon sat on opposite sides of the wall. A large portrait of a woman wearing a long, flowing evening gown hung over the roses. "Nice painting," Daniella said, looking at the portrait that seemed to have been painted in the early 1800's.

"That's my great-grandmother," Brant said.

"Ummm hmmm," Daniella murmured, admiring the winding staircase. Plush, thick beige carpet covered the stairs, blending with the gold staircase rails. Instead of going upstairs with Brant, Daniella stuck her head inside the study. Cream-colored furniture, a glass cocktail table and end tables adorned the room. Huge brass lamps covered with cream-colored shades the size of small sallite dishes sat on the glass tables. A tall ceramic white tiger sat in the corner near the fireplace and on the walls hung a couple of abstract originals. A bookshelf on the left wall was filled with books.

"Dannie," Brant called down from the top of the stairs to her.

"I'm on my way up," Daniella said, closing the door to the study, climbing the stairs to the second floor.

"Sleep well," he said, moving away from the bedroom door that Daniella assumed was hers. His eyes shifted to her lips and for a moment Daniella thought he was going to kiss her. He didn't. Instead, Brant turned on his heels and moved down the hall to his room.

"Good night," Daniella said. It was just as she had thought, their trip to Georgia was all business, she mused, watching Brant move down the hall to his room. She kicked off her shoes and discarded her clothes. Daniella sat on the gold-cushioned bench at the foot of the brass canopy bed and opened her suitcase to get her comfortable gown and housecoat.

Instead of her cotton gown and the other clothes she'd laid out for Beverly to pack, Daniella pulled out of the suit case black silk and satin sleepwear, lace red and black panties and matching bras, short-shorts, waist-length shirts and stretch jeans that were designed to show her figure. *I'm going to choke Beverly,* Daniella fumed as she examined the thong bathing suit. The only piece of luggage that Beverly had followed her instructions on was the garment bag. Beverly had packed Daniella's sundresses and a suit.

Daniella took a quick shower and crawled into bed, letting the sounds of crickets and croaking frogs lull her to sleep.

The next morning, before Daniella and Brant visited the facilities, they sat at the table in the gazebo in the center of the pond and ate breakfast. Daniella sipped iced coffee and ate toast, while Brant had a healthy plate of hash browns, sausage, and toast.

"I swear, Dannie, I don't see how you make it until lunch eating that light," Brant said, biting into a sausage.

"If I eat a heavy breakfast, I'll be asleep before lunch," Daniella said, setting her glass down, gazing out at the bed of purple, blue, and red tulips near the pond. She cast a glance at Brant, watching him attack his breakfast. Just watching him eat made her heart warm. "Who're we house-sitting for?" Daniella asked Brant out of curiosity.

"It's mine." Brant stopped chewing and looked at her. "Like it?" Brant asked and went back to his food.

"Yes, I think it's a lovely home," Daniella said. "But it's too far in the woods for me," she added.

"I come here at least twice a year," Brant said, finishing his breakfast.

"And do what?" Daniella asked, glancing at the thick, green pine forest that sat in the back of the pond.

"It's a good place to chill out and think," Brant said, pushing away from the table.

"Uh, I guess it's different strokes for different folks. I personally like to hear a siren and see a traffic jam every once in a while," Daniella said, setting the dishes on the tray.

The corner of Brant's mustache tipped into a smile.

"Let's get to work, so we'll be finished by noon. Because afterward, I have to find you a traffic jam." Brant grabbed the tray of dishes and they moved across the walkway that led away from the gazebo.

Finally, they reached the house. Daniella and Brant went inside and washed the dishes. Brant washed and Daniella dried. While Daniella was placing the last plate in the cabinet, Brant stood behind her, so close she could feel his body brush against hers.

"Are you sure you wouldn't want to live here?" he asked, moving closer to her.

Daniella pushed the cabinet doors shut and closed her eyes before turning around to meet Brant's gaze. Brant gathered Daniella in his arms and lowered his head, his lips brushing Daniella's lightly.

"No."

Brant kissed her.

Daniella circled her arms around Brant's neck and stroked the back of head. Suddenly, they pulled away.

"Let's go," Brant said, smiling down at her.

Daniella sat on the truck's seat beside Brant, enjoying the breeze that cooled the hot summer air. She inhaled the scent of pine and the pleasant aroma of Brant's heady cologne.

"God, it's peaceful," Daniella said, observing the low, fluffy white clouds that reminded her of cotton candy.

"I knew you would like it," Brant said, glancing at Daniella from behind his sunglasses, while he found a static-free radio station.

Country music and the soft roaring of the truck's motor were the only sounds she heard. Added to those sounds were the crunching gravel underneath the truck's tires as Brant drove down the lane.

"This place is a soul soother," Daniella said, thinking of all the stressful moments she didn't miss back in Jersey: no phone calls from Ray's insane associate threatening her to give him money that she didn't have, no crowds rushing to go nowhere, no traffic jams, no foggy pollution to inhale. It was just the quiet, easy hum of a tractor in every other field. At the end of the thick, green pines that lined the sides of the roads and every other half mile or less, set a brick home with a yard big enough for a football field.

It wasn't long before Brant drove up into the yard of a huge, faded house that looked as if it had once been painted white.

"This yard needs sod," Brant suggested, cutting the truck's engine.

"Yes, it does," Daniella agreed, noticing the sandy yard that was sprinkled with brown rocks and a few sprigs of weeds.

The house was in need of cosmetic repairs. Most of the windows were broken. The deteriorating doorstep sagged under Brant's weight.

"Be careful." Brant reached out and helped Daniella over the weak plank.

The house wasn't as damaged as Daniella thought, once she got inside. Her job was to work with ventilation and other systems that would make the house comfortable to live in. Daniella groaned. How boring she thought. Instead of decorating the homes, she would be making sure that the electrical space was adequate and that the ceilings were okay for the ductwork.

"The wood is good," Daniella said, tapping her fingers against the sturdy walls in the living room.

"Yeah," Brant said, taking out his pad and pencil, taking notes.

It was past noon when Daniella and Brant finished making preliminary designs for the house.

Daniella slid into the truck beside Brant.

"I'm ready for you to show me that traffic jam," Daniella said, half-teasing and half-serious.

"All right," Brant grinned, turning the key in the truck's ignition.

"I don't believe that there's another car within five miles of here except for yours." Daniella glanced out at the corn and cotton fields across the road.

"I can show you better than I can tell you," Brant said, driving out onto the black paved road that headed to the main highway.

Daniella wound the truck's window down and

inhaled the fresh, unpolluted country air. Peace and quiet, Daniella thought, realizing that the only sound she heard was the soft hum of a tractor in a field next to the road.

Daniella closed her eyes and rested her head against the soft leather seat.

About fifteen minutes later, the scent of fried fish and the sounds of laughter and automobile horns floated through the warm southern air.

"Child, please. Traffic and people?" Daniella said, surprised that people actually lived here. "Where are we?" she asked Brant.

Brant chuckled. "Every year, the town gives a community gathering," Brant said, pulling his truck in between two parked cars. "It's sort of like a homecoming, only there's no parade," he said, cutting the engine.

"Ummm hmmm," Daniella said glancing out of the truck's window, straining to see more of the festivities. She could hear a crowd cheering a baseball game that was in session. Vendors stood behind carts covered with red and yellow umbrellas selling hot dogs, barbecue lunches, cold sodas, lemonade, and beer.

"Are you hungry?" Brant asked Daniella while opening the truck's door for her to get out.

"Yes," Daniella said, checking out her surroundings, as they walked to the hot dog vendor. They bought hot dogs and covered them with mustard and ketchup before they walked to the baseball park.

Daniella and Brant sat on the second bench behind the chicken wire, ate their hot dogs and watched the game.

"Strike one!" Daniella heard the umpire yell. The

call reminded her of her childhood days when she played softball for the Dusty Devils.

"So, what, this team plays people from other towns?" Daniella asked Brant, getting interested in the game.

"I think they're playing a softball team from Miami," Brant said, gazing out into the field.

"Child, please," Daniella said, laughing. It never occurred to her that the backwoods would be entertaining.

"Okay, I'll take Miami and you can take Georgia," Daniella said, settling back on the bench.

"You think Florida will win?" Brant gave her a side glance.

"Yeah," Daniella replied with assurance.

When Florida scored a point, Daniella rose from her seat.

"Yes—yes—yes!" she screamed, standing up, pumping her fist toward the sky.

Brant chuckled, pulling Daniella down beside him.

"I think you better cheer under your breath, Dannie. We're sitting in the Georgia section."

"Ooh, why didn't you tell me before I start cheering?" Daniella asked Brant, glancing around at the sour faces, staring at her.

As it turned out, the two teams tied scores and it seemed like it would take hours before the scores were untied.

"Let's get out of here," Brant said, reaching in his pocket for the truck keys.

"Brant, I'm not ready to go back to the house," Daniella said, wishing they could stay until the game was over.

Brant's response to Daniella's request was a grin.

He slipped his arm around her waist and they walked to the truck.

A couple of miles later, Brant parked on the side of a street in front of another large gathering. People were standing out on the grass in front and on the side of an old building that looked more like a shack than a club.

Nevertheless, Daniella was thrilled. Music mingled with conversation and loud laughing filled the air.

People were sitting on cars, the grass, lawn chairs, and tailgates of trucks.

"What's this?" Daniella asked Brant, excited to see more people.

"The people that didn't go to the game, came here," Brant said, holding Daniella's hand as they moved to an outside bar.

Brant ordered two beers and handed one to Daniella. Just as Daniella took a sip of her beer, she heard a woman's voice behind them.

"Brant Parker," the woman said, "give me a hug." The young woman wrapped her arms around Brant's waist and kissed his jaw.

"Hi, Sandra," Brant spoke to his cousin. "Dannie, this is Sandra Williams," Brant introduced the women.

Sandra nodded, and smiled at Daniella, "Hi," she spoke, then turned back to Brant.

"I know you're going to stop by and visit with Greg before you go back to New Jersey," Sandra said, suggesting that Brant visit her husband.

"I can't Sandra," Brant said. "The next time I'm down here I'll stop by and visit with you and Greg."

"Okay, I'm not taking no for an answer the next time you're in town," Sandra said, she turned to

Daniella and smiled. "It was nice meeting you," Sandra said before she headed across the grass.

Daniella nodded.

Before Brant could explain Sandra and her actions to Daniella, a slow song from the jukebox floated from the speakers. Brant took Daniella's beer and set both their drinks down on a nearby bench. He pulled Daniella into his arms and they rocked slowly to the sultry love song.

Daniella rested her head against Brant's chest. It felt good being in his arms, inhaling his cologne, feeling his heart beat against hers. It was as if they were one individual, one soul, one mind and heart. Brant lowered his head, capturing Daniella's lips with a slow-burning kiss.

Daniella and Brant danced, laughed, and talked until the crowd begin to thin around one A.M. It had been a long time since she'd had that much fun.

It was after two when she and Brant drove back to the house.

Once inside, Daniella headed up to her room, leaving Brant standing in the foyer. As soon as Daniella showered and slipped into her gown, Brant knocked on her bedroom door.

Without speaking, he gathered Daniella in his arms and smothered her lips with hot, sizzling kisses. Her heart pounded with passion and desire, making her blood inch through her veins like a slow-burning fire.

With her mind made up to let Brant love her and to love him in return, to enjoy the passion and to unleash her desire, Daniella kissed Brant's lips, his chin, and made a trail down to his bare chest.

Brant slipped his fingers under the thin straps of Daniella's gown, peeling away the silk, exposing her round breasts. He inclined his head, kissing the hollow of her neck, and slowly his mouth settled on top of her breasts, torturing Daniella with his hot, firm lips.

Just as he lifted her in his arms, a flash of Ray Spencer's face trekked across Daniella's mind. She untangled herself out of Brant's embrace and leaned against the dresser for support. The passion and desire that Daniella felt for Brant slowly diminished.

"No, Brant," Daniella said, reeling from the desire she had felt for him.

"What's wrong, Dannie?" Brant wanted to know.

"Nothing," Daniella said, avoiding his eyes.

"If I've done anything to offend you, tell me," he said, looking at Daniella.

"It's not you," Daniella said, pulling on her gown.

"Then what it is, or who is it?" Brant said, swirling Daniella around to face him.

"I'm not ready," Daniella said, inclining her head, so Brant wouldn't see the tears in her eyes.

"In other words, you don't feel the same way that I feel about you." Brant said, forcing her to look at him.

"I need more time, Brant," Daniella said, trying to keep the words from sticking in her throat.

"Time for what—to get over a dead man?" Brant inquired.

Daniella cast Brant a brief glance. The tears that she had tried to swallow, rolled freely as she watched the angry, hard lines around Brant's mouth and smoldering fire in his eyes. At that moment, Daniella hated Ray more than she'd hated him two years ago. She had allowed him to ruin her quest for love, and because of him, she probably would lose the only man that she had grown to have feelings for in a long time.

Brant dropped his hands to his side, and moved back. "When you want me as much as I want you, let me know." With that said, Brant left her room, leaving Daniella with her tears. She wanted to run to Brant and explain her actions. But it was too late. She had lost what friendship she had with Brant and nothing else mattered.

CHAPTER 12

Brant sat at the drafting board checking the designs on the Georgia project that he and Daniella had worked on together. It had been exactly one week since he and Daniella returned from Georgia and things hadn't been the same between them since. Daniella had avoided him as if he had a contagious disease. She talked to him only if she had to.

Brant leaned back in his stool and glanced at the clock on the wall above his work area. It was past nine A.M. and Daniella still wasn't at work. It wasn't like her to miss work, Brant thought, getting up and going to his desk and dialing Joyce's extension.

"Joyce, did Dannie call this morning?" Brant asked.

"Yes, she did. She said she wouldn't be in because she didn't feel well," Joyce informed Brant.

"How sick is she?" Brant rubbed a finger across his mustache. If Daniella was ill, he wanted to know.

"I don't know. She didn't say," Joyce replied.

"All right," Brant said, hanging up. He dialed Daniella's home number. After the about the fifth ring, the answering machine kicked in.

"Dannie, this is Brant. I heard you weren't feeling well. Give me a call."

Brant replaced the receiver and walked over to the window. He wondered if Daniella had been harassed last night by the phone stalker. Maybe she hadn't gotten any sleep, he thought, pushing his fingers in the top of his jeans' pocket, and gazing out at the stone fountain.

It was unusual for Daniella not to feel well, Brant thought. She was strong and healthy. The only thing he'd ever known Daniella to suffer with were her sinuses. However, the mild illness never kept her from work. Daniella popped a pill and in no time, she was feeling good.

Maybe she's trying to quit because she doesn't want to be around me. Brant played with that idea for a while. He knew for a fact that she didn't want him. Daniella had proven that point while they were in Georgia. So why did he insist on trying to make her understand that they were right for each other?

Brant crossed the room and sat on the edge of his desk. He knew the answer to that question, and sprinkling on the tail of that conviction came the idea that Daniella probably thought he wanted her for his bed partner.

Oh God, don't let Daniella think that, Brant thought, going back to his work.

After work, he planned to go to Daniella's house and have a serious talk with her. For some reason, the lines of their communication had become tangled.

Around five-thirty, Brant finished his work, and checked his phone messages. He didn't want to worry about returning messages while he was convincing Daniella that he really wanted her—and not for some quick romp between the sheets. He knew Daniella was a stubborn woman and making her see the light about his true feelings could take half the night.

Brant punched the numbers to his home voice mail and listened to his messages.

"Brant, this is Glenda. I was going over the books for the Women's Charity Ball and noticed that you hadn't bought your ticket or given a donation. Would you like for me to stop by and pick up the check and drop off your ticket?"

No, Brant thought, making a mental note to remind Joyce to purchase his ticket and to give her a check for his annual donation. He went to the next message.

"Hey Brant, this is James. I needed another pallet of grass for the backyard, so, I went ahead and ordered it, and had the company send the bill to you. I hope that's all right."

Brant nodded. He liked James. The man worked hard and best of all, he had restored the house on the lake to look almost new.

Brant placed the receiver on the cradle. He took out his checkbook and wrote a check for his donation and ticket for the charity ball, before he grabbed his briefcase and headed out to his truck. On his way down the corridor, he met Tyrone.

"I'll see you later, bro," Brant said.

"I'll catch up with you later at the gym." Tyrone told Brant.

"No, I have something I've got to take care of," Brant said.

"All right, take it easy," Tyrone said, going inside his office.

Brant stopped by Joyce's desk and stuck his head in the door.

"Joyce, pick up my ticket for the Women's Charity Ball and while you're there, leave this check with the treasurer," he said, referring to Glenda, who volunteered her accounting skills a few evenings a week.

"Will do," Joyce replied.

Brant walked outside into the late afternoon. He couldn't remember the last time he'd left his office early. But it was important that he and Daniella have a long talk.

When he got to Daniella's house, her Jeep wasn't in the driveway. Brant didn't give much thought to that because Daniella sometimes parked in the garage.

Brant got out and rang her doorbell. When she didn't answer after a few rings, Brant headed back to his truck. Just as he slid behind the wheel, Grace Mills stepped out on her porch. The elderly woman held her small dog in one arm and slowly raked her long, red manicured nails across the animal's small head.

Grace Mills stepped off her porch and ambled down her walkway, stopping at Brant's truck.

"Dannie left a few minutes ago. And if you ask me, she seemed very upset," Grace said.

For the first time since Brant had met Mrs. Mills, he appreciated her desire to mind other people's business.

"What do you mean, she seemed upset?" Brant inquired, wanting to know the exact state Daniella had been in when Grace last saw her.

"Oh, I spoke to her and she didn't speak. She

seemed to have been in another world," Grace said, moving away from the truck and walking across the street to the park.

Oh my God, Brant thought, backing out of Daniella's driveway, and heading home. He'd find something to do while he worried about Daniella and waited for her to return home. Brant decided that he'd go for a swim once he got home. Swimming usually helped release his stress.

While Brant drove home, all sorts of scary thoughts crossed his mind concerning Daniella and the stalker. Suppose the person had ordered Daniella to meet him or her someplace? What if Daniella wasn't able to protect herself from the stalker with that tube of Mace she carried around with her on her key chain? As Brant allowed his imagination to run amuck, all sorts of horrible thoughts splintered across his mind as to what could happen to Daniella. Brant's apprehension for Daniella deepened and he realized that he had to take action.

Brant figured he needed to call Jerry. Jerry's firm often worked on cases for Nick. From what Nick had told Brant, Jerry was the best PI in town.

Brant pulled into his driveway, and went inside his house. From the scent of roast beef coming from the kitchen, he knew the housekeeper he shared with his parents was making dinner. Brant walked into the kitchen before going to the study to call Jerry.

"Hi, Karla." Brant lifted the lid off the pot, and looked in.

"Hello, Brant." Karla slapped his hand. "Get your nose out of my pot."

Brant chuckled, and headed out to the study to give Jerry a call.

"Hey, what's up Jerry?" Brant said.

"You got it, homeboy. What's going on?" Jerry responded.

"I have a problem I need you to look into," Brant said, dropping down in his chair at the desk.

"Yeah?" Jerry said.

"I think Dannie is being stalked and I need you to find that person, and whatever you do, don't say anything about this to her," Brant said.

"Oh—ah Brant, I don't usually discuss my cases with other people, but I'm working on that for Dannie," Jerry said.

"Really?" Brant asked, tapping the edge of the desk. He had been right. The call that Daniella received that night had been a serious threat. "How long have you been looking for this person?" Brant asked, his concern for Daniella's safety growing.

"Not long. I've been working on the case in between my other work, mainly because I was doing it as a favor to Daniella."

"Forget the favor, Jerry. Hire as many people as you need to find this guy and send me the bill," Brant said. "And no matter what, Jerry, stay with her."

"All right. I'll do that," Jerry said.

Brant and Jerry discussed Daniella's problem for a while longer before Brant hung up and went upstairs to put on his swim trunks.

Brant sank down in the cool pool water. He had done the right thing to hire Jerry to protect Daniella.

CHAPTER 13

Devastated from the news that Jerry had told her ast evening and the note that the stalker had slipped hrough her mail slot, Daniella drove to Brant's 10use. She had made the tormenting decision to tell 3rant that she was resigning from her position at 'arker's Art.

Daniella had read the stalker's note at least ten imes that day. The words were etched in her mind.

> *Daniella,*
> *Don't worry about paying me the money. Your boy-friend will take care of your debt.*
> *Signed,*
> *Your friendly bill collector*

Daniella had sat in her house all day, nursing her ears. Her insides felt as if they were tied in knots.

Each time the phone rang, she had trembled. Finally, she had turned the ringer off.

The part that disturbed her the most was the fact that Brant had been good to her. He paid her well, and all she could repay him with was pain. Daniella resolved that she had to resign from Parker's Art if she wanted Brant to keep his wallet safe from Ray's greedy friends. She had to warn Brant of the danger he was in—and what made the situation worse, she was the cause of it. Ray had been a menace to her when they were married, and he was an even bigger menace to her dead. Daniella remembered how Ray didn't give a second thought to bilking anyone out of their money. She was certain that Ray's friends had the same attitudes.

Daniella parked in front of Brant's Four Seasons retreat-style home. As she moved closer to the two-story gray stone-front house, she knew she would get through this disaster and her life would go on. As much as she loved Brant, she couldn't allow her problems from the past to burden him. Daniella rang the doorbell and stepped back.

Karla opened the door. She resembled a nurse wearing a white uniform and white rubber-sole shoes, Daniella thought as she glanced at the maid. Daniella swallowed. "I'm here to see Brant."

"Do you have an appointment?" Karla studied Daniella.

"No, do I need one?" Daniella asked.

"Wait here, I'll see if he's available," Karla said, her red lips curved into a faux smile.

Daniella placed one hand on her hip and the other on the edge of the double-wide door, and glanced out at Brant's perfectly manicured yard. Beds of crimson carnations nestled close to short, green grass. Miniature hedges lined the side of the garage and a small evergreen pine that reminded Daniella of an artificial Christmas tree stood to the right of the house. While she observed Brant's perfect surroundings, she knew she was doing the right thing. This was her battle and she would fight it without further involving Brant.

Brant opened the door, hurling Daniella out of her retrospections.

"Baby, are you all right?" Brant pulled Daniella inside.

Daniella cast a brief glance at Brant's handsome face. The worried lines around his mouth made him appear older than his thirty-six years. She lowered her gaze, letting her eyes trail over Brant's naked rock-wide chest. Finally, she noticed the thick, blue towel wrapped around his waist, covering his narrow hips and strong thighs.

"I have something important to tell you," Daniella said, recognizing the dreadful truth. After this meeting with Brant, she wouldn't see him again.

"Let's go in here," Brant said, taking long strides through the foyer, and to the great room, closing the door behind them. He sat on the edge of the beige leather sofa. "Dannie, what's going on?" Brant pulled Daniella down beside him.

For a moment, Daniella stared out past the glass sliding doors that led to the patio and out at the pool. If only her life were as peaceful as the pool's water, she would be thankful. But Ray Spencer had taken it upon himself to ruin her life.

"Everything is wrong, Brant," Daniella spoke quietly, willing herself not to cry.

"Tell me about it." Brant took Daniella's chin

between his thumb and forefinger, forcing her to look at him.

Daniella lowered her glance. She had come to him, willing to resolve their relationship. Working with Brant and loving him was not good for his health and his finances.

Suddenly, Daniella felt weak from the stress she'd been under all day. "I—I can't work for you anymore," she said, folding her hands in her lap, waiting for Brant to respond. The silence between them was like the Georgia fog—thick.

"What brought this on?" Brant asked her, his voice seemed edged with steel.

Daniella glanced at Brant then looked away. Once again, she struggled with tears that threatened to fall any minute. *Don't cry. He might feel sorry for you,* she told herself.

"I had a meeting with Jerry," Daniella said, controlling the tremble in her voice with an iron will.

"All right, but what does Jerry have to do with you not working for me?" Brant pretended that he had no knowledge of Daniella's dealings with Jerry.

"It has everything to do with us working together." Daniella forced herself to stay calm.

"I don't understand," Brant said.

Daniella got up and walked over to the glass sliding doors. She might as well tell him and get it over with. "It's my ex-husband's associates," Daniella said, and bit down on her lower lip before the distorted predicament she had gotten Brant into spilled from her. She explained it all without stopping, while Brant stood before her, listening in silence.

Daniella told Brant the phone calls were from Ray's friend in Florida. She told him how Jerry was working to find Ray's friend. Finally, she took the note from her purse and laid it in Brant's hand. Brant read the threatening note that linked him to the stalker.

"This note is not a reason for you to resign," Brant said, his brows pleated into a frown.

"Yes it is. Why should you get involved with my problem?" Daniella replied.

"It's my problem now. If you want to take a few days off, feel free, but don't quit, Dannie," Brant said.

"I can't do that. The stalker is watching me. If he sees that I'm no longer working for you, maybe he'll forget about wanting your money," Daniella said.

Brant walked over to the wall and slammed his fist against the wood so hard, a picture shook.

"I don't believe that you're letting that ex-husband of yours run your life from the grave," Brant shot back. "If Ray's friend finds me before Jerry finds him, I'll deal with the guy," Brant said.

"No—you can't do that," Daniella said, the tears that she'd been fighting spilled from her eyes. If Brant was hurt, she would never forgive herself.

"Dannie, why is it so hard for you to accept anything from me?" Brant asked, going over and gathering Daniella in his arms. The towel he was wearing slipped from around his waist.

Daniella shivered from the touch of Brant's bare chest, and cried even harder for the man that she could never have.

"I have to go," she said.

"Dannie, I love you and you know there's nothing I wouldn't do for you," Brant said, wiping a tear that rolled down her cheek with the side of his thumb. Daniella raised her head and through teary eyes, she gazed at Brant. She loved him, too, and she would do anything to protect him.

"I'll fax you my resignation tomorrow."

"You can't do that," Brant said.

"Yes, I can," she said, choking back fresh, salty tears.

Brant cursed, raking his finger through his hair.

Daniella cast her gaze down, and sniffled.

"Thanks for everything, Brant," Daniella said, moving toward the door.

"Baby, don't do this," Brant pleaded.

"It's for the best," Daniella said, glancing over her shoulder.

Brant picked up the towel and wrapped it around his waist and went after her.

"Marry me, Dannie," Brant said, stepping in front of her, blocking her from walking out the door.

Daniella stopped. She couldn't believe that Brant thought marriage was the answer to her problem.

"No," Daniella said, pushing passed him.

Brant moved closer to Daniella, touching his fingers to her waist.

"Dannie, I can be there for you."

Daniella turned to Brant then. She was determined to stick to her promise to protect him. She wiped her eyes and glanced at him.

"I said no, and I meant it," she said evenly and walked out into the warm summer evening.

"Dannie," she heard Brant call out to her.

Daniella continued to walk to her Jeep. She didn't look back for fear she would run to Brant and stay with him forever. The tears clogged her throat and she couldn't have spoken if she wanted to.

Daniella slid behind the wheel of her Jeep, and wiped her blinding tears.

Finally, she drove home. She sat down on the sofa in her living room, and allowed the hot, salty tears to slide down her cheeks. Resentment for Ray and his nefarious friend welled up in her. She hated them all for forcing her to end a wonderful relationship with a man that she truly loved. She hated them for forcing her to quit the job that she loved. Most of all, she hated Ray for reaching out from the pits of hell, reeking havoc in her life again.

Daniella rocked back and forth weeping gut-wrenching tears. This was the second time that Ray had wrecked her life. While she sobbed, her mind wandered to the past. A past that she would rather leave buried, but like Ray, who had left a trail of misdeeds behind to haunt her, Daniella's past was like a dark phantom.

Daniella met Ray at a birthday pool party in Fort Lauderdale, Florida. Ray had been the most hand-some man she'd met since she'd been vacationing in Florida. He had a pecan-tan complexion, beautiful pearl-white teeth, and Lord he had smelled so good. His slacks hung just right over his slim hips, and when he introduced himself and smiled at her, Daniella knew Ray was the man she wanted. However, a small voice in her mind warned her to move with caution. Daniella ignored it and lost her good levelheaded senses. Ray seemed sincere. He called her the next evening as he had promised. He was a successful accountant. He owned property and he had studied and graduated from Florida International University some years ago.

One month after they met, when Daniella was back

in New Jersey, Ray started visiting her every weekend. He wired her chocolates and flowers. He bought her expensive jewels. But what impressed Daniella about Ray was that he insisted that they wait until they were married before they made love.

Daniella introduced Ray to her parents. They objected to her seeing Ray Spencer, telling Daniella that she really didn't know him. They wanted Daniella to date him another year before getting married. As usual, Daniella allowed her stubborn streak to turn a deaf ear to her parents. They were too protective of her, and she was old enough to make her own decisions.

Daniella got up and went to the kitchen and snatched a paper towel from the roll. If only she would've listened to her parents, she thought, blowing her nose. She hadn't listened to anyone, not even to herself.

Daniella returned to the living room and flopped down on the sofa as the memories of her wedding day flooded her mind.

The wedding was a lavish one to say the least. The night before the wedding, Daniella and Beverly sat up until midnight. They laughed, talked, and reminisced about their childhoods. Beverly reminded Daniella that if her marriage didn't work, Brant was willing and waiting. Daniella had made a face. No man would ever take the place of Ray Spencer. How foolish she had been. Daniella sniffled at the harsh realities of her marriage as the memories reeled back. Her and Ray's wedded bliss lasted about four years after the honeymoon. Ray began to spend long hours at work. That was his story to Daniella. By the second year

Ray wasn't coming home at all and when he did, he was quiet and smelled of liquor.

Daniella begged him to go with her to see a counselor. Of course Ray refused. He didn't need anyone telling him how to run his life. He was the man of his house and he would do what he wanted, when he wanted to do it.

When Daniella couldn't stand the way her life was going, she called Beverly, and they would talk for hours. Beverly soothing Daniella, and Daniella hoping that she was doing the right thing by staying with Ray. After all, didn't all married couples have problems? Too soon, the fake world that Daniella had built fell apart. Ray stopped paying his share of the bills. When Daniella confronted him with the problem, he smirked, reminding Daniella that her daddy was a wealthy man and that she could get the money from him. Besides that, Ray had added that he only married her because she was to inherit a small fortune when her father died. He didn't love her and if she tried to divorce him, he would stop her. Daniella didn't know how Ray intended to do that, so she decided to find out everything she could about him. What did he do at night? Was he working? She called Jerry.

Shocked at the information that Jerry had found out about Ray, Daniella called her lawyer, and filed for divorce. Ray Spencer had a woman in Miami, and a three-month-old son. He had property that he had no intention of Daniella finding out about and he ran with a crowd of crooks. Ray's buddy had a lump sum of money that he had no doubt swindled some poor person out of and gave it to Ray to hide in Ray's bank account.

The day the divorce was finalized, the judge awarded Daniella half the property, half of Ray's finances, and gave the condo to her as well.

Daniella sold the property and the condo and put the money toward her retirement plan and invested in mutual funds and stocks. She moved back to New Jersey and was lucky to get her old job back at Parker's Art.

Daniella gazed out the window of her town house. The streetlights snapped on, casting a ghostly shadow into Daniella's living room. She didn't bother to get up and turn on her lights. It was comfortable sitting in the dark reliving her miserable past.

The sound of the doorbell drew Daniella back to the present. She got up and looked through the peephole before opening it for Beverly.

"Come in," Daniella said in a coarse whisper.

Beverly flipped on the light, took one look at Daniella, and held up her hands.

"You don't have to go into it. Brant is at the house now." Beverly walked with Daniella over to the sofa and they sat.

"You didn't have to come over, Bev, I'll be all right," Daniella said and wiped tears from her eyes.

"I overheard Brant telling Tyrone that you didn't want anything to do with him. So—I figured I'd come over and see how you were doing," Beverly said.

"I think it's best that Brant and I go our separate ways," Daniella said, not going into detail about why she had chosen not to see Brant again. The less her friends knew about the predicament she was in, the safer they were, she thought.

"Are you sure?" Beverly asked, giving Daniella a quick glance.

"Yes," Daniella said.

"Is there anything that I can do?" Beverly asked.

"Just be my friend," Daniella said.

Beverly smiled. "I will always be your friend, Dannie."

Daniella sniffed and nodded. She was quiet and lost in her own private world.

CHAPTER 14

Brant Parker had finally arrived in his career. He had everything a man could wish for, except the woman that he wanted. Brant sat in the easy chair, crossed one leg over the other, folded his arms across his chest and accepted the fact that Daniella Taylor didn't want any parts of him.

As thoughts of his nonexistent love life came to mind, Brant glanced at the accolades on the wall in his study. If only his love life was as rich as his career, Brant contemplated.

However, he would keep his promise to protect Daniella whether she wanted him or not.

Brant changed the channel on the television. The news was depressing. Sirens outside a house where a man was holed up inside for robbing a bank was the highlight of the news. Brant groaned, thinking of his situation with Daniella and her ex-husband's friend.

He switched channels. The Marlins had won the baseball game, and so had the Yankees.

Brant punched the remote-control button, cutting the power on the television. The colored light that had lit the room, faded to black, leaving the study dark and soundless.

Brant closed his eyes and shifted in his chair. He had played life's game like it was a sport too. For years, he had won. He had thanked God for his good fortune and had taken nothing for granted. But it seemed that he was losing the game now. He needed balance. Someone to share his love and comforts with.

For the first time in his life, Brant felt like giving up. He couldn't do that. He would go on with his life.

Brant was closing his eyes, hoping he could take a nap, when the phone rang. He got up, walked over to the desk, and pressed the speaker button, so he could speak to whomever it was without holding the receiver.

"Brant here," he said, sitting on the edge of the desk.

"Hey, guy, you went into hibernation or something?" Evelyn's voice came across the line.

"No, I'm chilling," Brant said.

"Look, I'm going to The Café tonight. Why don't you come with me." Evelyn said.

Brant pushed his hands in his pants' pockets and slid off the desk. "I might," he said, remembering that every weekend The Café had a live blues band.

Evelyn giggled. "What do you mean, you might. You're either going or you're not," she said.

Brant was quiet for a minute. He didn't have anything else to do. He might as well enjoy himself.

Besides, he hadn't been very polite to Evelyn the night he'd found Daniella at the club. He hadn't hesitated to put Evelyn in a cab and send her home.

"All right. I'll meet you at The Café around ten," Brant said.

"Ten o'clock?" Evelyn asked. "I would like to get a table close to the front."

"Evelyn, I have something to do." I'll meet you at The Café at ten."

"Okay," Evelyn said.

Worrying over Daniella made him tense.

Brant turned the lamplight on in the study and went upstairs. He pulled on gray sweats and a white, sleeveless T-shirt. He checked his gym bag for his boxing gloves. He pulled on a pair of sweat socks and sneakers and headed out to his truck. A good workout on the punching bag was usually the perfect cure for his frustration and tension.

As always, the gym was crowded on a Saturday evening. Brant gave his membership card to the receptionist and waited for her to run it through the computer. While he waited, he could see through the window into the main area of the gym past the treadmill machines and exercise bikes. The punching bag was free.

Brant waited impatiently while the receptionist checked his membership not wanting to miss the chance at releasing the tension that had built up within him.

Brant walked up to the punching bag, took his red leather gloves from his gym bag, and held out his hand to the attendant who had come over to assist him.

Brant raised his fist and tapped the hard, black

punching leather, as if testing to see how much pounding it could take. He stepped back and popped the bag with more force, making it swing back and forth. Brant bounced back, and waited for the bag to swing to him. He whacked the bag again harder, bobbing and weaving, smacking the bag. Each time his fist connected with the leather, he reminded himself how hurt he was because he had ruined a good thing with Daniella.

It all happened when he and Daniella were in Georgia. He popped the bag. He had been anxious. He rammed his fist into the bag again, bobbing and weaving. He could've waited, but he had let his starving libido get the best of him. Brant stepped back, wiped the sweat from his face with the back of his glove, and took a permanent stance. Instead of bouncing away from the heavy bag, he let it come to him.

He had felt like a fool that night in Georgia. Daniella had rejected him. Brant slammed his fist into the leather. *Whack!* He had gotten over his inferiority complex hadn't he? *Thwack!* Apparently not. When Daniella refused to love him, it had felt as if she had reached into his chest and snatched out his heart. *Bop!* He slammed the bag again. Did he stop wanting her? No. He went ahead like a fool and asked her to marry him. *Thwack, thump . . . thump.* It had served him right that Daniella had rejected him. But not even that had stopped him from loving her, Brant mused, as he punched the bag harder. Brant had hired Jerry to protect her, when he knew the woman didn't want him. Brant pounded the heavy bag with his fists. It was clear to him now that Daniella had married her husband, and her promise until death do us part, had meant everything to her.

Brant staggered away from the punching bag, wiping the sweat with the towel that the attendant had left on the bench. Breathing hard, Brant sank down on the steel bench and lowered his head, resting his elbows on his thighs. He realized that beating the stuffing of the punching bag wouldn't make Daniella care about him. But somehow, pounding the leather eased the pain and made his days and nights a little easier to get through.

Brant rose and signaled for the attendant to help him out of his gloves, when he saw Jerry coming toward him.

The attendant untied one of Brant's gloves and pulled it off.

"Thanks," Brant said, untying the other glove with his free hand and sitting back on the bench.

"What's up?" Jerry said, sitting down beside Brant on the bench.

"Nothing much. Did you find that guy?" Brant asked Jerry.

"Not yet. But I'm this close," Jerry said, measuring a space between his thumb and forefinger. That guy is playing games with me, man," Jerry said.

"Is Dannie all right?" Brant glanced out in the gym. He didn't want Jerry to see the pain he was feeling.

"Yeah."

"Stay with her Jerry," Brant said.

"I will. I'm taking her out tonight."

"Good," Brant said, knowing he could trust Jerry. After all, Jerry and Daniella had been friends since they were children, Brant thought, banishing any thoughts he might have of Jerry winning Daniella's heart.

"And another thing, man," Jerry said, standing up. "I told Dannie that I would take her to the Women's Charity Ball next Saturday night, but I don't know if I can," Jerry said. "I have a meeting. It depends on how long the meeting lasts."

"Dannie isn't speaking to me, but I'll keep an eye on her," Brant said.

James Amour stood in the aisle next to the dumbbell equipment and watched Brant walk out of the gym. James pulled his thick ponytail. He had a few more hours of work to do on Brant's house before it was complete.

In a few days, I'll be a brand-new man. Yes sir buddy, James thought and grinned

CHAPTER 15

Daniella sat across from Jerry in the dimly lit café, listening to a middle-aged blues singer cantillating love songs as if he had read her mind and knew all about her broken heart.

Daniella tapped the rim of her wineglass and silently wished that she was out with Brant instead of Jerry.

Since a relationship with Brant was impossible, Daniella dismissed her wishful thinking and pulled at the hem of her short, red spaghetti-strapped dress.

Jerry had made it clear that tonight he would not discuss her case. They were going to drink, dance, and have fun. Feeling safe with Jerry as her protector, Daniella agreed.

Finally, the band played a fast tune and Daniella asked Jerry to dance with her. As Jerry turned her around on the dance floor, she began to feel like her old self: happy and flirty with not a care in the world.

Daniella's carefree attitude soon lost its luster when she saw Brant walk in and sit at the table with the woman he'd been with the night that she'd ruined her dinner party.

The band stopped playing and Daniella was suddenly tired and wanted to go home.

"Come on, Dannie, we just got here," Jerry said, walking with Daniella back to their table.

"I know that," Daniella said, trying to think of a lie to convince Jerry why she wanted to go home.

Daniella pulled out her chair and sat down, as she gazed around the room, seeing Tyrone and Beverly near the back. She stole another glance at Brant and his female friend.

He sure didn't waste any time, Daniella thought, reminding herself that it hadn't been long since Brant had asked her to marry him. The nerve of him, Daniella fumed drinking a sip of her wine. She set the glass down and continued to cast brief glances at Brant and the woman.

When Brant laughed, the woman laughed. Daniella rolled her eyes to the ceiling.

Puleeze! Daniella imagined that if Brant jumped off a cliff, the woman would jump too.

"What's wrong with you, Dannie?" Jerry asked her, following Daniella's gaze.

"Oh," Jerry said.

"What's that supposed to mean?" Daniella asked Jerry.

"Nothing." Jerry grinned, holding up his hands as if he had to defend himself from Daniella.

"Excuse me," Daniella said, pushing away from the

table as gracefully as she could. "I need some air," she said, uncomfortable with the jealousy that raked at her heart. She had experienced many emotions over the years, and she had to admit that she had also experienced a mild case of jealousy. But tonight, the green-eyed monster was showing no mercy.

"I'm going with you," Jerry said, standing.

"No, you're not," Daniella said, glancing at Brant again. This time her gaze locked with his. Daniella grabbed her purse and headed to the ladies' room instead of outside as she had planned.

She leaned against the vanity counter and took several deep breaths, as if this exercise would stop her heart from pounding too fast in her chest. It was making her sick to think that Brant was loving another woman.

A few seconds later, Beverly walked into the ladies room. "Dannie, I'm glad you decided to get out of the house," Beverly said, setting her purse down on the vanity counter beside Daniella.

"Hi, Bev," Daniella said, going to sit on the small love seat.

"Dannie, are you feeling okay?" Beverly asked her girlfriend.

"Yes . . . no . . . I don't know," Daniella said, tinkering nervously with her purse.

Beverly gave Daniella a knowing look.

"You want to talk about it?" Beverly asked her.

Daniella rose from the couch in one fluid move.

"I don't understand men not even a little bit," Daniella said. "To hear Brant tell it, he just loves me with all his heart. He'll do anything to make me happy," Daniella fussed, taking Beverly's hand, leading her to the ladies' room entrance. She looked in Brant's direction.

"Just look at him," Daniella said, tilting her head in the direction of Brant and his date.

Beverly smothered a giggle.

"I thought you didn't want him," Beverly said.

Daniella gave Beverly a side glance.

"Shut up, Beverly," Daniella said, and strutted out of The Café. She needed that fresh air after all.

Daniella stood outside the club with some other people, inhaling the summer air and trying to banish any thoughts of Brant Parker from her mind.

But she couldn't forget him. It had felt good being close to him. To inhale his cologne, to feel his thick mustache against her cheek, her neck . . . Daniella shut out the memories.

Suddenly, Daniella smelled the scent of liquor mixed with the scent of cheap men's cologne. Slowly she turned to face her stalker. He was tall, dark, and wore a curly perm.

"I been looking for you ever since I saw you in Zelda's," the man said. "Yeaaah, you're a beautiful creature all right."

"Excuse me," Daniella said, moving away from the man, unsnapping her purse with one hand and reaching for her Mace with the other.

"You don't have to get bent out of shape," the man said, grinning, showing his gold teeth.

"Get out of my way," Daniella moved toward The Café's door.

"See, that's what I say about you women. Always whining about you can't find a man and when a good man like myself tries to talk to you, your nose gets out of joint."

By the time Daniella inched halfway to The Café's door, Brant and Jerry were outside.

Brant stepped in front of the man, preventing him from walking behind Daniella.

"You got a problem?" Daniella heard Brant ask the man. She didn't hear the man's answer. Jerry pulled her toward his car.

"Stop, Jerry," Daniella said, struggling to free herself from Jerry.

Jerry opened his car door and stood in front of Daniella until she got in.

"I'll be right back," Jerry said, going to Brant, as if Brant needed his help.

Daniella stared at Jerry, then settled her gaze on Brant. She could hear Brant asking the man all sorts of questions, like who was he, where did he come from, why was he talking to Daniella. The crowd began to gather and Daniella had never been so embarrassed in her life.

The crowd thickened and Daniella lost sight of Brant, Jerry, and the man. It seemed like Daniella sat in Jerry's car for thirty minutes before Brant slid in beside her.

Daniella lowered her lids, drew in a deep breath, and let it out slowly.

"Where's Jerry and what do you want?" Daniella asked Brant, who was looking at her through slanted eyes.

"Jerry is taking care of that guy, and I'm taking you home," Brant said.

"I came here with Jerry and I'm leaving with him. You got that?" Daniella asked, and settled back against the soft leather seat. Watching the woman that she'd seen sitting at the table with Brant walk across the parking lot.

"You have a choice. You can walk to my car, or I can throw you over my shoulder and carry you," Brant said.

Daniella shifted her eyes to Brant's. His light brown eyes looked as if they were brimming with fire.

Daniella decided that it was in her best interest to go with Brant without putting up a fight.

She slipped off the seat and walked with Brant to his Mercedes, making certain that she didn't complain when Brant opened the door for her.

Daniella stared out of the window on the way home. If it wasn't for the jazz disc playing, they would've ridden to her house in silence. Daniella stole a glance at Brant out the corner of her eye. His jaw was hard and relentless, and he was looking straight ahead.

Finally Brant drove into Daniella's driveway.

"Who was that guy?" Daniella turned to Brant and asked before getting out of the car.

"He was some drunk . . . and what were you doing outside anyway?" Brant answered Daniella's question and asked a question all in the same breath.

"The last time I looked, it was a free country," Daniella shot back.

"And the last time I looked, a crazy man was stalking you," Brant retorted.

"That doesn't mean that you're supposed to question every strange man that talks to me," Daniella said.

"Don't worry about it," Brant said, opening his door.

Daniella got out of the car and glanced over her

shoulder, noticing a strange, black automobile parked at the curb near the park.

"Uh, that's strange. I didn't think that cars were allowed to park on that curb this time of the night," Daniella said, climbing the steps to her town house.

Brant shrugged and reached for Daniella's house key. He twisted the key in the lock and walked inside Daniella's house, turning on lights and checking the doors, going upstairs and checking the windows.

"Brant you don't have to do that," Daniella said, when Brant came back downstairs.

"Dannie, for some reason you don't seem concerned about your safety," Brant said, leaning against the edge of the staircase.

"I care about what happens to me. But Brant you have to be careful too. You didn't know whether the man had a weapon or not," Daniella said, kicking off her shoes. "Besides, it's not like I need a guard."

"I guess you're right. After all this guy is a friend of your ex-husband's and you do know him. Right?" Brant's voice sounded cold.

Shocked at Brant's suspicion of her, Daniella turned to him. "I only knew one of Ray's friends."

Brant folded his arms across his chest as if he were shutting Daniella out.

"Why can't you get Ray out of your system, Dannie?" Brant inquired.

Daniella felt hot tears burning her eyes. Her feelings for Ray were dead and buried long before Ray was.

"I don't understand what makes you think I love Ray," Daniella said, moving over to the living room window, turning her back to Brant.

"What am I supposed to think, Dannie?" Brant asked.

"I don't know, I can't control your thoughts," Daniella argued.

"I love you, but I'm not competing with a ghost." Brant moved over to her and stood behind her.

The jealousy that had clawed at Daniella's heart earlier welled up in her.

"You love me?" Daniella's voice rose to a new level. "Why don't you save that line for that woman you were with tonight."

"I can explain that," Brant said.

"Oh, sure you can. You've been explaining that woman for weeks." Daniella's voice rose another fraction. It was like Brant's words had breathed life into the green-eyed monster.

Brant placed his hands on Daniella's waist.

"Dannie . . . it's not what you think," Brant tried to explain his casual friendship with Evelyn.

"Don't touch me," Daniella said, blinking back tears. Each time she thought that she was over Brant, her heart seemed to break a little more.

"Dannie . . ."

Daniella whirled around and went to the door and opened it wide. Warm tears rolled down her cheeks.

"Get out of my life. Get out of my house and don't come back!" Daniella said, holding the doorknob, waiting for Brant to leave.

Slowly Brant walked toward her. His mouth was set in a hard line. His eyes seemed to smolder with pain.

"Good luck, Dannie." Brant stood before Daniella gazing at her face. It seemed to Daniella that Brant was designing a mental picture of her in his mind.

Brant stepped out onto the porch.

Daniella slammed the door. She made it to the sofa and laid down. The tears that had flowed freely stopped. She was numb. She had lost her job and her love. Somehow, she would get through this ordeal, even if she had to move to another state.

Sometime in the early-morning hours, Daniella dozed off and slept. Around ten o'clock Sunday morning, she woke and decided that she needed to go to church.

Daniella went upstairs, and took a hot shower. She wouldn't allow herself to think about the confrontation she'd had with Brant last night. She needed to pray. She dressed in a dark blue suit, a matching wide-brimmed hat and went to church.

When Daniella walked into church, the minister was announcing the title of his sermon, Love. Daniella sat on the front seat, not because her parents were sitting there, but because she didn't want to miss a word the minister had to say.

"Brothers and sisters, sometimes we don't know how to accept love," the minister said, clearing his throat. Daniella held her head down. The minister was beginning to step on her toes.

"Sometimes a person tries to show you their love in many ways and you just don't get it. Eveually, that person will leave you. Love is a wonderful thing to have, brothers and sisters, so let's love one another, let's stop being mean to one another . . ."

Daniella began to say a silent prayer, asking God to forgive her for being mean to Brant. *God, if Brant is the man for me, give me one more chance with him.*

When the sermon was over, Daniella spoke to her

parents briefly, giving them each a hug. She refused their dinner invitation. She had things to do, like finding Brant. She hoped she wasn't too late.

Daniella drove down the street a block from the church and dialed Brant's number on her cellular.

The maid answered and informed Daniella that Brant was out of town and wasn't expected to return until the end of the week or the first of the next week. Disappointed, Daniella thanked the maid and hung up.

The next week, Daniella kept herself busy so she wouldn't think about Brant. She didn't call the maid service to clean her house. She cleaned it from top to bottom. She did laundry, she ironed, and by the end of every day, she was too exhausted to think.

From time to time, Jerry stopped by to give her the details on the case.

"Don't worry, Dannie, I'll get him," Jerry said one evening when he stopped by Daniella's with her favorite Chinese food.

"Jerry, you've been catching this man all summer. I don't want to hear about him again until he's behind bars," Daniella told Jerry, while they ate stuffed Chinese mushrooms.

"I'll present him to you on a silver platter, behind bars," Jerry joked.

Daniella didn't think it was funny. If one of Ray's friends got his sticky fingers on Brant's money, she was certain that Brant would hate her forever.

Saturday morning, Daniella opened her mail. She threw the letters marked Occupant and the sales papers into the garbage and opened the letters. The last letter was from Brant. In the folds of the letter lay a check. Daniella gasped at the amount.

Dear Dannie,
    I hope that you're doing well. I can imagine that you're keeping busy, so I won't waste your time. Since we won't be taking that trip together, I've sent you a check. I hope you enjoy your trip to whatever island you choose.

Love,
Brant

A tear dropped from Daniella's eyes onto the letter, smudging the blue ink. Daniella got up and snatched a paper towel from the rack. Just like the minister said in his sermon, Brant was tired and he had left her.

Daniella went upstairs and took a hot bubblebath. By the time she finished applying her makeup, removing the big pink sponge rollers from her hair, and dressing in the short black evening dress she had bought for the Women's Charity Ball, Jerry was ringing her doorbell.

Daniella walked outside and locked her door. In her heart, she wished that Brant was escorting her to the Women's Charity Ball instead of Jerry.

"I'm ready whenever you are," Daniella said.

CHAPTER 16

Brant stood next to the entrance of the hotel's Charity Ballroom and spoke to Tyrone about his trip to Georgia and the progress he'd made on the project. He asked Tyrone if he could monitor the Georgia project while he took a short vacation.

While Brant discussed business with Tyrone, he glanced through the sea of black-and-white tuxedos and sequined, short and floor-length gowns, looking for Daniella.

When Brant didn't see her, he wondered if she had changed her mind about attending the Women's Charity Ball. *Maybe she thought she would run into me,* Brant mused in between his conversation with Tyrone.

Then he remembered that Jerry had mentioned a meeting that he was attending that evening. If Jerry was still in his meeting, Daniella wasn't at the ball.

Brant could barely concentrate on his meeting in Georgia for thinking about Daniella. He wanted to hold her again, smell her subtle, sweet scent. He wanted to call her and see how she was doing. Each time he picked up the phone to call Daniella at the end of his day, he remembered the last fight they'd had and figured she meant it when she had thrown him out of her house.

Finally, Brant saw Daniella standing on the balcony. "I'll talk to you later, Tyrone," Brant said, moving toward the terrace to Daniella. While he was in Georgia, he'd made up his mind that he needed a long vacation. He needed time to rest and get over Daniella. But first he had wanted to say good-bye to her.

Brant nodded at a few people he knew as he moved slowly across the room, priming himself for another one of Daniella's rejections, knowing that she was going to hurt his feelings the minute he approached her. He didn't care anymore. He had tried to stay away from her, keeping himself too busy to think. So exhausted at night that at his very best, he took a shower and slept until morning. Worst of all, he had interrogated an intoxicated man, giving him the third degree. None of it had mattered. Daniella was through with him, it was as simple as that.

Brant moved out onto the terrace. He pushed one hand into his pocket and rubbed the back of his neck with his free hand. He stood in the doorway, studying her, shifting his eyes to her soft, long neck. He wanted to reach out and touch the curly strands that dangled loosely at the nape of her neck. His eyes slowly shifted to her bare back. He lowered his gaze to where the back of the black party dress snapped at her waist. A shudder raced through Brant. What was he going to do without her? She had been the only woman he had ever loved.

"Nice, isn't it," Brant said, moving beside Daniella, leaning against the rail, gazing out at the Manhattan skyline. The lights flickered against the Hudson resembling rubies, emeralds, and diamonds.

Daniella looked at Brant. "Ummm-hmmm. How have you been?"

Brant shrugged. "I've been okay," he exaggerated. He had been miserable.

"And you?" Brant asked, shifting his gaze to Daniella's lips.

"I'm fine," Daniella said. *You need to stop telling lies, Miss Thing,* a small voice in the back of Daniella's mind said.

"That's good," Brant said, leaning his back against the rail so he could look at Daniella. "I'm going away for a while, Dannie."

"For how long?" Daniella asked, turning to Brant.

"I don't know. Three, maybe six weeks. It depends on how I feel. I need to rest, Dannie," Brant said.

"What about your work?" Daniella inquired.

"Tyrone will look after everything," Brant replied. "If you decide to work for the company again, the interior design job is yours." Brant doubted that Daniella wanted the job now.

"Okay." She inclined her head. "So . . . where're you going?" Daniella asked.

Again, Brant could have sworn he heard concern in Daniella's voice. But he was sure he had made a mistake. Just like he had made the mistake to love her. He shifted against the railing.

"I'm going someplace where the fishing and swimming are great," Brant said, hoping that when he returned from his vacation, Daniella would have gone on with her life. In the meantime, he had no intention of living in the same town with her while it was happening.

His cellular phone rang. Brant reached inside his tux pocket, took out the phone, and answered it.

"I'll be right over," Brant said to the caller.

"Take care, Dannie," Brant said, gazing at Daniella.

"Are you leaving for your vacation tonight?" Daniella asked.

Brant pushed his hands in his pockets. "No," he said, backing away from her before he lost control and kissed her. "I'm leaving in the morning." Brant gazed at Daniella, shifting his eyes to her lips, remembering how sweet she was. Then without another word, he walked through the ballroom door, and faded into the crowd.

Brant went home to change out of his tux, before going to the lake house to settle up with James Amour. James had told Brant that he was leaving tonight. His work at the house was finished. While driving to the house, Brant allowed thoughts of Daniella to come to mind. She was an independent woman. He seriously believed that Daniella would starve before she borrowed money for food. Nevertheless, he loved her for those very reasons.

Brant parked in the driveway of the house and used his key to enter.

"James," Brant called, walking through the living room. The house smelled of stale liquor and beer and cigars.

"I'm in the kitchen," James called out to Brant.

Brant moved through the living room and into the kitchen.

"Where are you, James," Brant said, walking farther into the kitchen.

"I'm right here," James said, stepping out from behind the door, swinging an iron pipe at Brant's head.

Brant ducked, staggered back, knocking over a chair.

"Man are you crazy?" Brant asked James.

"No. I hate guys like you," James said, still holding the iron pipe. "You got everything a man wants."

"What 're you talking about?" Brant said, staring at James.

"You got money. You even got my ex-wife," James said, moving toward Brant.

"Ray," Brant said, realizing that Daniella's ex-husband was alive. "Do you know what you've put Dannie through?"

"Yeah, and I don't care," Ray said, swinging the iron pipe at Brant's head.

Brant ducked and ran into him, grabbing Ray and wrestling him to the floor. The pipe fell from Ray's hand and rolled on the floor, as Brant slammed his fist into Ray's body. "If you hurt Dannie, you'll live to regret it," Brant said, standing up, dragging Ray up from the floor by his shirt collar. Brant pushed him against the wall.

Slowly, Ray moved away from the wall and grabbed the iron pipe. He swung at Brant again. Brant ducked, tripped over the chair and fell to the floor, hitting his head against the steel tool box.

Everything around Brant went black.

* * *

James Amour tied Brant's ankles and wrists with the rope he had ordered from the supply store when he had ordered the pallets of grass. He couldn't take any chances with Brant Parker. If Brant recovered before James made his phone call to Daniella, Brant might beat him again.

James took Brant's cellular from his pocket and went outside. As James walked along the edge of the lake, he called Daniella's home number. When he didn't get an answer, James went inside, and took Brant keys from his pocket and drove to Daniella's house. He parked a few town houses down the street from hers and wrote a note. Then walked to her house and slipped the card through her door's mail slot.

Brant Parker had paid him well, but once James found out that Brant wasn't a poor man, he wanted some real money.

"I think Brant can afford to break me off that amount," James said to himself as he walked back to Brant's pickup, thinking about the amount he planned to request for Brant's safe release.

CHAPTER 17

Daniella sat at the table in the hotel's ballroom with Beverly, Tyrone, and Jerry, listening to the president of the Women's Charity Ball announce the grand total of monies that the committee had raised.

Grace Mills clutched the podium as if she might fall after reading the grand total.

"Ladies and gentlemen, I would like to thank you all tonight for your generous donations." Her voice trembled with pride as she spoke to the audience.

"Once again, you have assisted our children in having an opportunity to attend the colleges of their choice."

The crowd applauded.

Grace smiled. "I have been the president of this club for many years and this is the first year that we have reached our goal. Thank you, thank you," she said, beaming as the crowd applauded again.

"I promised myself tonight that I wouldn't make a long, boring speech because I know that all of you want to get up and dance and talk to your friends. So, without further ado, enjoy yourselves."

Just as Grace Mills stepped off the stage, Jerry's phone rang. Jerry flipped the top and answered it. Daniella watched Jerry from the corner of her eye, nodding his head while he listened to the party on the other end.

When the call was over, Jerry leaned over to Daniella.

"We have to go," Jerry stated.

"Jerry, the party just got started," Daniella said, realizing that Jerry's phone call had been an emergency. "You go ahead, I'll get a taxi home."

"Dannie, my assistant just told me that a guy has been hanging around your house. We believe it's the guy who's been stalking you. Do I have to tell you more?" Jerry asked Daniella.

"Oh my God," Daniella said, pushing away from the table. "Beverly, I have to go, but I'll call you tomorrow."

"Is everything all right?" Beverly asked Daniella, shifting her glance from Daniella to Jerry.

"Yeah, I have to leave. Duty calls," Jerry said, as if he didn't want anyone to get alarmed.

"Well, Dannie, we can give you a ride home," Beverly said.

"No, she's coming with me," Jerry interrupted before Daniella could say anything else to Beverly.

Daniella went over and said good night to her parents before she and Jerry left the hotel.

"Are you sure you have to leave?" Annie Mae rose from her chair, pressing her hands over her pale blue sequined gown.

"Yes, Mother. But I'll call you. I'm thinking of taking a trip to the Bahamas and I would like to use the house," Daniella said, smiling and kissing her parents' cheeks. Daniella was careful not to let on to her parents that she was being stalked.

"You can stop by and get the key anytime," Jake said, smiling at his daughter.

Daniella thanked her parents and walked out with Jerry.

Black fear ripped through Daniella as Jerry and Daniella drove to her town house.

"Jerry, what's going on?" Daniella asked.

"Brant hired a guy to repair his house at the lake. We believe he's the same guy that works at the gym. So one of my men and I set a trap for him," Jerry said.

"What kind of trap?" Daniella asked, her fears swelling in her as she thought of the close contact Brant had made with the stalker.

"We followed a hunch and decided to discuss Brant's finances and holdings in the gym's locker room," Jerry said. "We also mentioned that Brant loved you."

"You did what?" Daniella turned to Jerry.

"Dannie, it's all right. Brant knew about it," Jerry assured her. "He told us to do it."

"I don't believe this," Daniella said. "Is that the reason the stalker left the note saying he was going after Brant?" Daniella inquired. She was more concerned for Brant's saftey than ever now.

"Jerry, if Brant is hurt, I will never forgive you," Daniella said.

"Dannie, we had to use Brant for bait. The stalker figured you didn't have all the money he wanted. Why else would he take so long to come after you."

"I swear, Jerry, I will never forgive you." Daniella's brows pleated into a frown.

Jerry pulled up in Daniella's driveway and cut the engine and the lights. He and Daniella got out of the car at the same time, running to her house.

"Give me your key," Jerry said, taking it from Daniella. He unlocked the door, walked in, and picked up a note off the floor, then switched on the lights.

"What does the note say, Jerry?" Daniella asked as calmly as she could, but her stomach was knotted with fear.

"Let me check the house out first, Dannie," Jerry said, examining Daniella's town house, with Daniella trailing behind him.

When Jerry was sure the house was safe, he read the note.

"Good. Now all we have to do is wait," Jerry said, handing the note to Daniella.

"What, Jerry, what?" Daniella snatched the index card from his hand. She read the horrible message and sank down on the sofa. "Oh my God." Daniella felt as if every muscle in her body had turned to rubber. Her hands trembled, and from deep inside, she felt a sob, making its way to her throat.

She read the dreadful note for the second time.

Dannie,

 I have Brant. If you want him healthy again, he'll have to pay. Don't even think about calling the cops. I'll talk to you soon.

Signed,
Your friendly bill collector

Stunned from the horrible news, "Why, Jerry . . . why?" She choked back tears. She couldn't let Ray's awful friend rob Brant.

"Dannie, all we can do now is wait for that lowlife to call you," Jerry said, getting up and going to the phone. "I think I'd better call Nick."

Daniella hugged a throw pillow, rocking back and forth. *Please God don't let him hurt Brant,* Daniella prayed.

Jerry called Nick. They talked for a minute or two before Jerry hung up and sat next to Daniella.

"Dannie, I'll turn the phone's speaker on so you can hear when the call comes in. I'll do the talking," Jerry instructed Daniella.

Daniella was so nervous, she couldn't talk. She nodded. If Brant was hurt, she would never forgive herself. She knew this was not her fault, but she blamed herself. She thought if she resigned from Parker's Art, she would protect Brant from Ray's friend.

The phone rang. Daniella jumped up.

"I've got it," Jerry said, motioning Daniella to stay seated.

Jerry walked over and pushed the speaker button on the phone. "Yeah?" he said.

"Who is this?" James asked Jerry in an annoyed, smothered voice.

"Jerry," Jerry said, waiting for a response.

"Well . . . well if it's not the private eye. Some detective you are. You couldn't even save your boy," James said.

Daniella gasped.

Jerry glanced at Daniella over his shoulder and placed his finger to his lips. "Shhh," he mouthed.

"Where's Daniella?" James wanted to know.

"She's not here and what do you want, man?" Jerry asked.

"For starters, I want you to give Daniella a message. You tell her that I have her lover, and she ain't getting him back until I get his money," James said.

"Let me speak to Brant." Jerry sounded frustrated.

"Brant ain't in no position to talk, but when he feels better, I'll think about letting him talk to you."

Jerry placed his hands on his waist, pushing his jacket back, exposing his gun and black leather holster.

"All right. How much money do you want?" Jerry said to Brant's kidnapper.

James told Jerry in no uncertain terms the amount he wanted.

Daniella gasped louder this time.

Jerry gave Daniella a side glance.

"Be quiet," Jerry mouthed.

"We can't get that kind of money tonight," Jerry said.

"Monday morning around ten o'clock will be fine with me. And if you think about calling a cop, Daniella can forget about seeing her boyfriend again." James hung up.

"Damn him!" Jerry said, just as Daniella's doorbell rang.

Jerry opened the door and let Nick inside the living room.

Nick stood in Daniella's living room. His honey complexion seemed to have darkened with anger. He looked at Daniella through cold black eyes. As Nick walked toward her, Daniella carefully observed Brant's brother. He was almost the exact image of Brant, except for the graying temples of his short, wavy black hair.

Nick walked over and squatted in front of Daniella. His eyes were steel, cold, and hard.

"If one hair on my brother's head is harmed, I'm going to see to it that you never get out of jail," Nick said to Daniella.

An icy fear swept through Daniella. Unable to speak, Daniella gazed into Nick's cold black eyes and nodded.

"Leave her alone, Nick," Jerry defended Daniella.

"You're trying to tell me that she didn't know that this creep was out to get Brant." Nick rose from his squat.

"No, it's not my fault," Daniella said, defending herself.

"Sure you did. You pretended to love my brother, then lured him into a trap." Nick stated his case as any good lawyer would do. "You set Brant up. It's as simple as that," Nick said to Daniella.

Daniella glared at Nick. She couldn't believe that he was accusing her of something she had no control over.

On top of that, Nick was speaking to her as if she were a common criminal.

Daniella rose from the sofa. She had wallowed in her fears for too long. It was time to take charge of her and Brant's life together. She didn't know how things would end, but she knew that she couldn't allow Ray's friend to destroy Brant.

While Jerry and Nick argued back and forth about who was at fault for Brant's abduction, Daniella took her purse and walked through the kitchen and out to the garage. Just as she opened the garage door and got into her Jeep 4x4 and started backing out onto the street, Jerry and Nick ran outside.

"Dannie, where're you going?" she heard Jerry call out to her.

Daniella didn't stop to tell Jerry that while he was talking to Brant's kidnapper, she had heard the sound of water splashing and motors roaring in the distance. She wasn't sure if the sounds of motors were coming from an automobile or a boat, but she was willing to believe that the call came from Brant's lake house. Daniella turned onto the street and headed toward the lake. She didn't worry about Jerry or Nick following her. She knew they would wait for the next call from the stalker. At least she hoped they wouldn't follow her. At the moment, her concern was about keeping Brant safe.

She rounded the curve and jug-handled off to the road that took her to the lake. *God let me be right about this,* she prayed silently. *And please keep me and Brant safe.*

If Ray's friend was as devious as Ray, Brant is in trouble, Daniella thought as she rounded another curve. Daniella caught a glimpse of the white church where she'd prayed just last Sunday and listened to the minister's sermon on love. She sped up.

It wasn't long before Daniella parked at the edge of Brant's neighbor's property. Daniella got out of her Jeep and started walking. The sound of her high heels clicking against the sidewalk echoed against the darkness. Daniella tiptoed. She didn't see Brant's car or his truck. She moved closer to the house. The lights in the front rooms were on.

Daniella decided to look in the backyard for Brant's truck. Sure enough, Brant's white pickup was parked next to the lake.

Oh my God, Daniella thought, praying that Ray's friend hadn't dumped Brant's body in the lake. She walked around to the front.

Daniella tiptoed up the front steps to the house and punched the doorbell. Seconds later, the door opened. Daniella thought her heart had leaped to her throat. She braced herself to keep from falling. For a moment, thick, black silence stood between her and Brant's kidnapper.

"Ray!" Daniella stared at her ex-husband.

"Well, well." Ray gave Daniella a nefarious grin. "If it's not my widowed wife."

Daniella held Ray's gaze, staring him down. If Ray thought for one hot second that she was afraid of him, he would destroy her. Daniella bit down on her bottom lip and swallowed hard.

"I should've known this was one of your tricks, trying to make everybody believe you were dead." Daniella glared at Ray's beard, mustache, and thick ponytail.

"It worked," Ray said, still grinning.

"For a while. But your schemes always blow up in your face. You should be ashamed of yourself," Daniella said, straining to see inside the living room.

"Well, Brant is a nice guy. He loves to help stragglers and bums like myself." Ray's grin turned into a nasty smirk.

"Where is Brant?" Daniella stared at Ray.

"Do you have the money I asked for?" Ray asked.

"No."

"Then you can't see him. Or maybe you'd like to join him." Ray reached out, attempting to grab Daniella.

"Get away from me, Ray," Daniella said, taking a step back. She flipped the top on her key chain.

"Oh, I don't think so," Ray said, glancing at Daniella's keys. "What're you gonna do with those keys . . . stick me in my neck?" Ray reached for Daniella again and missed her.

"Yes," Daniella replied, pressing the top of the Mace container. She watched with pleasure as Ray crumbled to the floor, wailing like a wild, wounded animal. Daniella walked around him into the living room, then sprayed him again for good measure.

Once Daniella was certain that Ray was in no condition to harm her, she ran down the hall to check the bedrooms. When she didn't see Brant, Daniella looked inside the bathroom.

Scared half to death, Daniella ran to Ray.

"What did you do with him?" She watched Ray as he continued to thrash and wail.

From the kitchen, Daniella heard a low, muffled groan.

"Oooooh!" Daniella ran to the kitchen. "Oh my God," she ran to Brant. She knelt down beside him. "Brant . . . can you hear me?"

"Ummm—hmmm—u . . ." Brant groaned as if he were drifting in and out of consciousness.

Daniella touched the spot on Brant's head that was trickling blood.

"Oh God, don't let him die. Oh God . . ." Daniella started running around the room looking for a phone. The phone in the kitchen was out of order. She ran to the living room where Ray was in his own world of Mace.

"Oh thank you, God," Daniella said, remembering her cellular. She dialed 911. And ran to the kitchen for a knife to cut the rope on Brant's wrists and ankles.

"Oh my goodness. I have to call Jerry," Daniella said. She had been talking to herself like a crazy woman. She called Jerry at her home. "Jerry I'm at Brant's house on the lake."

"Dannie, what are you doing over there?" Jerry yelled.

"Shut up Jerry and get out here. I have Brant and I Maced Ray . . . I'm at the . . ." Daniella was almost incoherent.

"Ray . . . Ray Spencer?"

"Yes," Daniella screamed into the receiver and hung up.

Daniella ran to Brant and began sawing on the rope with the knife. By the time she cut the ropes, she heard an ambulance and police sirens.

While an officer questioned her, several policemen cuffed and dragged Ray to a car.

"May I have your name, please?" The officer asked Daniella, as she watched the paramedics lift Brant onto a stretcher, taking him to the hospital.

"Daniella . . . Taylor," she answered the officer, trying to control the tremble in her voice.

"Do you know these men?" The officer continued interrogating her.

"Yes."

"Miss Taylor . . . It is miss, right?"

"Yes."

"We'd like for you to come down to the station for more questions," the officer said.

"But officer, I didn't do anything wrong," Daniella said, fear of Nick's warning about sending her off to jail sent icy shivers to the pit of her stomach.

"We understand, Miss Taylor, but we need you to inform us on what you know about this crime."

"Yes," Daniella whispered.

"Officer Davis will drive you to the station," the policeman said, nodding his head toward the policewoman standing nearby.

Daniella felt as if she was going to faint as she followed the officer to her patrol car.

As she waited for the officer to close the door to the vehicle, she wanted to cry, but her tears seemed as if they had turned to ice.

As she waited for the officer to take her downtown for questioning, she watched Jerry, Tyrone, and Nick skid up to the curb of Brant's house. The air reeked of tire rubber.

"How serious is my brother's condition?" Daniella heard Nick ask the officer that had been questioning her.

"I'm not sure. Check with those guys over there," the officer said, gesturing to an attendant that was climbing in the back of the ambulance with Brant.

Nick gave Daniella a stony glance as he passed the patrol car on his way to the ambulance.

Right then, Daniella realized that even if she and Brant had a chance at being together again, his family would blame her for what had happened to him.

A few minutes later, the officer drove her to the police station for questioning. When they arrived at the station, Daniella asked if she needed a lawyer. The officer assured her that she didn't, but Daniella called her lawyer, Gloria Williams anyway.

Once Gloria arrived, Daniella explained the situation and problems that she'd had with Ray while they were married and how she thought that he was dead. She explained her relationship with Brant. After what seemed like hours of interrogation, Daniella was free to go.

Gloria extended her hand to Daniella. "I don't think you and your friend will have Mr. Spencer to worry about anytime soon," she said, shaking Daniella's hand.

"Thank God," Daniella said.

"Good night," Gloria said, leaving the room.

Daniella walked through the crowded police station and headed out to the parking lot when she remembered that her Jeep was at the lake. She called a cab from her cellular phone and waited to go to the hospital to see Brant. He had to be all right, she prayed, looking up and down the street, wishing the taxi would arrive soon.

She wasn't sure what she was going to say to his parents. She prayed that they wouldn't blame her as Nick had.

God, please let Brant be all right, Daniella prayed as she got into the cab and the driver sped off to Forest General following her instructions. As the cabdriver sped through the lighted streets, Daniella prayed for Brant. She had known people to be knocked unconscious and never recover. However, Brant had made sounds as she freed him from the ropes that Ray had tied him with. Tears settled in her eyes as she recalled how helpless Brant had been when she found him.

The cabdriver pulled into the visitors' parking lot at the hospital. Daniella paid the driver and ran inside the emergency room.

"Can you tell me how your patient Brant Parker is doing?" Daniella asked the nurse at the desk.

"Are you a family member?" the nurse asked Daniella.

"No . . . I . . . I'm a friend," Daniella said.

"I'm sorry, Miss, but I'm not allowed to give out any information unless you're a member of his family," the nurse said.

"Please, I have to know," Daniella begged.

"I'm sorry," the nurse said, and went back to her paperwork.

Daniella sat in the emergency room and worried. She refused to leave until she knew that Brant was going to be all right.

It wasn't long before Nick, Tyrone, and Jerry stepped off an elevator and walked into the emergency room.

Daniella hurried over to them. "What . . . is Brant going to be all right?" she asked.

Nick gave Daniella another stony gaze. "Yes, thanks to you."

"All right, you guys, don't start," Jerry said, looking from Nick to Daniella.

Tyrone shook his head. "Thanks Dannie for saving my friend."

The doctor came over and interrupted the conversation.

"We ran tests to see if Mr. Parker has a concussion.

At any rate, we're keeping him overnight for observation," Daniella heard the doctor tell Nick.

Nick nodded.

"Does he have a room yet?" Daniella asked Nick after the doctor had gone to look after another patient.

"He's in Room 203," Nick said.

"Can I see him?" Daniella asked Nick who seemed reluctant to let her near his brother.

"Yeah," Nick finally said.

Daniella left the men standing in the emergency room and took the elevator up to Room 203. She stepped off the elevator and hurried down the corridor, searching for the room number. When she found it, she eased the door open and tiptoed inside.

With tears brimming her eyes, Daniella knelt beside Brant's bed. She touched the white bandage that was wrapped around Brant's head.

"Brant, sweetheart," Daniella whispered, unable to control the tears.

"Hmmm," Brant groaned.

The sound of Brant's helpless moan made Daniella cry even harder. She took a tissue from the nightstand next to Brant's bed and wiped her eyes.

"I'm sorry. Please don't leave me, Brant." Daniella placed her hand in Brant's open palm. Brant gave Daniella's hand a light squeeze.

Daniella sniffled and smiled.

"I love you," she whispered.

"Hmmm," Brant groaned again.

Just when Daniella rose from his bedside and leaned over to kiss Brant, Nick, Clara, and Mark walked in.

"I think it's time for you to leave," Nick said to Daniella.

Slowly Daniella turned to face her accusers. Nick was the only one staring at her. Clara gave Daniella a gracious nod. As she stood next to her husband, Daniella noticed that Clara Parker was still wearing her dress from the ball. The long low-cut, sleeveless black gown gave a perfect view of the diamonds circling her neck and wrist. Clara's eyes were soft as she looked at Daniella through long, black lashes. Her salt-and-pepper hair was rolled into a sophisticated bun, exposing her long diamond earrings.

"I'm so sorry dear, that you had to go through this," she said, looking at Daniella.

Daniella was almost at a loss for words. She hadn't expected Clara Parker to show her any sympathy.

"I'm okay," Daniella managed to say and looked at Brant.

Mark reached for Daniella's hand. "Thank you," he said. Daniella noticed the worry lines around Mark Parker's eyes. He seemed older than she'd remembered him being earlier that night at the ball.

"We're all a little upset, Dannie," Mark said. "We're thankful that Brant will be fine."

Daniella smiled through her tears, took one last look at Brant, and left his hospital room.

A week later, Daniella sat on the sandy beach of the Bahamas in the back of her parents' small cottage, soaking up the morning sun, while she read the latest *Essence* magazine. As she read the southern recipes, she couldn't help but remember how well Brant loved to eat. Daniella laid the magazine facedown on her stomach and stretched out on her yellow beach towel. She pulled her wide-brimmed sun hat over her face and closed her eyes.

Brant was a part of her past. She had been too frightened to love him and because of her fears, she had lost him. She wished him well and hoped that he would find a woman that deserved his love.

With that thought in mind, Daniella dozed off, drifting in and out of sleep, dreaming of Brant. She could smell his rich cologne, feel his hard, muscular body next to hers, his lips touching her face.

The dream was so real. Daniella woke up, removed her wide-brimmed straw hat and sat up. She opened her eyes and looked up. His legs resembled two tree trunks. His bikini swim trunks were filled to capacity, his broad hands rested on his narrow hips. Daniella shifted her gaze further up. *Lord don't let me be losing my mind, and please, God, don't let this be an apparition,* Daniella prayed as she allowed herself the freedom to check out the hunk standing before her.

Daniella glanced up into his face.

"Brant—How did you know I was here?" she asked, watching his mouth curve into a grin.

Brant dropped down beside Daniella before she could get off her towel, and covered her hand with his.

"Hi, baby." Brant chuckled under his breath.

"Oh my God," Daniella said, thinking that Brant hated her by now.

"Dannie, I have one question for you," Brant said.

"I'm sorry, Brant. I didn't know that Ray was alive."

"Forget that," Brant said. "Will you be my wife?"

For a while, Daniella thought she was going to faint from pure happiness.

"Yes . . . I will . . . but what about your family? Brant, your brother doesn't like me."

"Who asked you to be his wife, me or my brother?" Brant asked Daniella.

Daniella's heart gave the same familiar flutter, her legs felt weak. She couldn't stand if she wanted to.

"You did," Daniella said, smiling at him.

Brant pulled Daniella to him, covering her lips with his, giving her an iron-melting kiss.

He raised his head and looked deep into her eyes.

"Thanks for saving my life," Brant said, between kisses.

"Mr. Parker, does that mean you can't live without me?" Daniella teased.

"Exactly," Brant replied, pulling Daniella down onto his hard stomach. "I think we should get married while we're in the Bahamas. What do you think?" Brant asked.

Daniella wrapped her arms around Brant's neck and kissed him. "Are you sure you want to marry me?" She smiled at him.

"Why wouldn't I?"

Daniella shrugged. "Let's put all jokes aside Brant. I was the reason for a lot of your problems. If it hadn't been for me, you would've never . . ."

"Shh," Brant said, kissing Daniella lightly. "You worry too much. I know all about your marriage to Ray. Dannie, please don't compare me to him."

"I won't," Daniella replied.

"Whew! What a relief." Brant laughed.

"I love you," Daniella said, allowing Brant to lift her in his arms and carry her to the cottage.

Brant carried Daniella inside and dropped her on the bed, making her giggle.

"Would you like to make love now, or do you want to wait until you're Mrs. Brant Parker," Brant asked Daniella, raising his brows.

"Now," Daniella said in a sexy, sultry tone. She rose and slipped her fingers in the waistband of his swim trunks, pulling him down on top of her.

"I'm not playing with you, baby. This time, I'm not stopping," Brant said, getting up and going over to his luggage, taking out a foil package. He tore the pack with his teeth, opening it.

"Kiss me and shut up." Daniella grinned.

Brant kissed her—all over, making her blood inch through her veins like hot liquid. Finally when Daniella thought she was going out of her mind, Brant sank deep. Nothing else mattered. It was as if they were swimming among the ocean's currents, until they were forced to climb a mountain of hot, sizzling passion.

Brant trekked to the peak of their rocky private world—a world that Daniella never knew existed, a world that sent her swirling out of control as they tumbled to earth and back to reality.

Daniella laid in Brant's arms, savoring their love. She rose and kissed the tip of his nose.

"I love you," Daniella said again, and she meant it.

Brant dragged her closer to him.

"Prove it."

The day after Daniella and Brant arrived home, Daniella called Beverly and invited her to lunch. As they sat at their table in The Glow sipping ice tea and waiting for their orders, Beverly brought Daniella up-to-date on what had happened in Forest while Daniella was vacationing in the Bahamas. "First of all, you know everyone at work was talking about what happened to you and Brant," Beverly said.

"I believe you," Daniella said.

"In the staff meeting, someone said that they heard that Brant had a head injury and that he wouldn't be able to work again."

Daniella smiled and shook her head.

"Girl, Tyrone had a hard time correcting those rumors to the employees in the meeting."

"Uh, uh, uh," Daniella said.

"Several of the senior employees were threatening to take an early retirement." Beverly said.

"Why?" Daniella asked.

"Dannie, you know how some of the older employees are. Most of them are set in their ways and scared to death of change."

"Did anyone quit?"

"No," Beverly said. Once Tyrone informed the employees that Brant was fine and on vacation, they calmed down.

"Okay, I'm glad that no one quit," Daniella said.

Beverly leaned forward, propping her elbow on the table and rested her chin on the back of her hand. "Let me tell you what Glenda did. She came to Parker's Art and placed an order to have her house redecorated. I think I showed her twenty fabric swatches and she didn't like any of them. So, I finally asked her why was she wasting my time." Beverly said, sitting back in her chair, as the waiter set their lunches before them.

Daniella nodded and listened to Beverly. "What did she say?"

"Glenda wanted to know what had happened to Brant. So I told her she would have to ask him when he returned from his vacation. Then she wanted to know where he'd gone on his vacation," Beverly said.

Daniella smiled, and laid her napkin in her lap.

"You should've told her."

"Well at the time I didn't know that Brant was in the Bahamas until Tyrone told me later that evening. Even if I knew, I wouldn't have told Glenda," Beverly said.

Daniella stuck her fork into a small piece of lettuce and put it into her mouth. She chewed slowly as she listened to Beverly. "It might not have been a bad idea," Daniella finally said.

"And have her go to the Bahamas and spoil your vacation?" Beverly said.

Daniella shrugged. "She could've been a witness to our marriage."

Beverly dropped the napkin she was about to lay in her lap and held up one hand. "Wait a minute. I think I misunderstood you."

Daniella smiled. "No you didn't. Brant and I were married."

"For real Dannie?" Beverly said, looking at Daniella as if Daniella was joking.

"I'm serious," Daniella said.

Beverly leaned back in her chair and laughed. "Congratulations, girl."

"Thanks," Daniella said.

"But you guys could've had a wedding," Beverly said.

"To tell you the truth Beverly, I didn't want a wedding. So, Brant and I decided that we would have a dinner party and invite our friends and a few people from work.''

"Good. Tyrone and I were beginning to think that you and Brant were never getting married.''

Daniella and Beverly finished their lunch and promised to call each other and meet for lunch, since Daniella wouldn't be returning to work for another two weeks.

In the meantime, Brant sat at his desk and informed Tyrone that he and Daniella had gotten married while they were on vacation.

"Say that again?'' Tyrone asked Brant.

Brant grinned and looked at Tyrone. "You heard me. Dannie is my wife.''

"Whew! Tyrone looked toward the ceiling. Thank you.''

Brant laughed.

After a week of rest and relaxing and lovemaking, Daniella and Brant sent dinner invitations to their family, close friends, a few Parker Art's employees, and several people from the Business Council. Daniella and Brant had planned a dinner party for those that loved and liked them.

"We decided to surprise everyone,'' Daniella said. So when the guests get here, don't tell them we're married.''

"Surprise? Honey, I'm shocked.'' Beverly gave Daniella a hug.

Six o'clock that evening, the other dinner guests arrived. Jazz, white wine, and good conversation set the mood for the evening's dinner party in the Parkers' dining room.

Daniella and Brant had removed the long dining room table and set up several round tables covered with white lace tablecloths to accompany their guests.

"Dannie and I would like to make an announcement," Brant said, after they had finished dinner and were on the patio sipping wine and champagne.

"Oh don't tell me you got engaged," Nick said, interrupting his conversation with Monique long enough to give Daniella and Brant a disapproving glare.

"No, we got married," Brant said, pulling Daniella to him.

Mark and Clara expressed how happy they were for Daniella and Brant. Jake and Annie Mae couldn't stop beaming. Daniella had finally married a man that wasn't a thief. Joyce and Karen were just as shocked as Beverly and Tyrone had been.

Annie Mae and Clara each went over and gave Daniella a kiss. Jake and Mark slapped Brant on the back and shook his hand.

George held his champagne glass up.

"I hope you guys have lots of children, so I can sell you the biggest house in this town."

"All right, George, we'll do our best." Brant chuckled and gave Daniella a squeeze.

Finally, Beverly went to Daniella and wrapped her arms around her best friend again.

"I still can't believe you married that boy." Beverly said, half-laughing and half-crying.

Daniella hugged and cried with Beverly, until Brant came over and rescued his wife.

That night, after Brant's and Daniella's guests,

friends and associates had gone home, Brant slipped his arms around Daniella. They held each other close.

"Baby, you're the best thing that's ever happened to me," Brant said, smothering Daniella's lips with kisses.

Daniella's eyes misted with tears as she remembered how hard it had been for her and Brant to design their love.

"Sweetheart, I have no complaints."

Dear Readers,

Have you ever broke a promise to yourself and then realized that breaking that promise was the best thing that ever happened to you?

Daniella Taylor broke her promise to stay relationship free. She had a change of heart after working with Brant Parker. Daniella soon realized that breaking her promise was a mistake when a trail of unsupected terror threatens to destroy her life, her career and the man she loved.

Love By Design was a challenge and fun to write. I hope you enjoy reading the story as much as I enjoyed writing and creating the characters.

I would like to hear from readers. If you would like a reply please enclose a self-address stamped envelope. PO BOX 640084 Miami, Florida 33164-0084

Best Romantic Wishes,

Marcella Sanders

ABOUT THE AUTHOR

Marcella Sanders grew up in Georgia and lived in New Brunswick, New Jersey for many years before moving to Miami. She is a vocational teacher and enjoys reading romance novels. She lives in Miami, Florida with her family.

COMING IN JULY . . .

FIRE AND DESIRE,   (1-58314-024-7, $4.99/$6.50)
by Brenda Jackson
Geologist Corithians Avery, and head foreman of Madaris Explorations, Trevor Grant, are assigned the same business trip to South America. Each has bittersweet memories of a night two years ago when she walked in on him—Trevor half-naked and she wearing nothing more than a black negligee. The hot climate is sure to rouse suppressed desires.

HEART OF STONE,   (1-58314-025-5, $4.99/$6.50)
by Doris Johnson
Disillusioned with dating, wine shop manager Sydney Cox has settled for her a mundane life of work and lonely nights. Then unexpectedly, love knocks her down. Executive security manager Adam Stone enters the restaurant and literally runs into Sydney. The collision cracks the barriers surrounding their hearts . . . and allows love to creep in.

NIGHT HEAT,   (1-58314-026-3, $4.99/$6.50)
by Simona Taylor
When Trinidad tour guide Rhea De Silva is assigned a group of American tourists at the last minute, things don't go too well. Journalist Marcus Lucien is on tour to depict a true to life picture of the island, even if the truth isn't always pretty. Rhea fears his candid article may deflect tourism. But the night heat makes the attraction between the two grow harder to resist.

UNDER YOUR SPELL,   (1-58314-027-1, $4.99/$6.50)
by Marcia King-Gamble
Marley Greaves returns to San Simone for a job as research assistant to Dane Carmichael, anthropologist and author. Dane's reputation on the island has been clouded, but Marley is drawn to him entirely. So when strange things happen as they research Obeah practices, Marley sticks by him to help dispel the rumors . . . and the barrier around his heart.

Available wherever paperbacks are sold, or order direct from the Publisher. Send cover price plus 50¢ per copy for mailing and handling to BET Books, c/o Kensington Publishing Corp., Consumer Orders, or call (toll free) 888-345-BOOK, to place your order using Mastercard or Visa. Residents of New York, Washington D.C., and Tennessee must include sales tax. DO NOT SEND CASH.

LOOK FOR THESE ARABESQUE ROMANCES

AFTER ALL, by Lynn Emery (0-7860-0325-1, $4.99/$6.50)
News reporter Michelle Toussaint only focused on her dream of becoming an anchorwoman. Then contractor Anthony Hilliard returned. For five years, Michelle had reminisced about the passions they shared. But happiness turned to heartbreak when Anthony's cruel betrayal led to her father's financial ruin. He returned for one reason only: to win Michelle back.

THE ART OF LOVE, by Crystal Wilson-Harris (0-7860-0418-5, $4.99/$6.50)
Dakota Bennington's heritage is apparent from her African clothing to her sculptures. To her, attorney Pierce Ellis is just another uptight professional stuck in the American mainstream. Pierce worked hard and is proud of his success. An art purchase by his firm has made Dakota a major part of his life. And love bridges their different worlds.

CHANGE OF HEART (0-7860-0103-8, $4.99/$6.50)
by Adrienne Ellis Reeves
Not one to take risks or stray far from her South Carolina hometown, Emily Brooks, a recently widowed mother, felt it was time for a change. On a business venture she meets author David Walker who is conducting research for his new book. But when he finds undying passion, he wants Emily for keeps. Wary of her newfound passion, all Emily has to do is follow her heart.

ECSTACY, by Gwynne Forster (0-7860-0416-9, $4.99/$6.50)
Schoolteacher Jeannetta Rollins had a tumor that was about to cost her her eyesight. Her persistence led her to follow Mason Fenwick, the only surgeon talented enough to perform the surgery, on a trip around the world. After getting to know her, Mason wants her whole . . . body and soul. Now he must put behind a tragedy in his career and trust himself and his heart.

KEEPING SECRETS, by Carmen Green (0-7860-0494-0, $4.99/$6.50)
Jade Houston worked alone. But a dear deceased friend left clues to a two-year-old mystery and Jade had to accept working alongside Marine Captain Nick Crawford. As they enter a relationship that runs deeper than business, each must learn how to trust each other in all aspects.

MOST OF ALL, by Louré Bussey (0-7860-0456-8, $4.99/$6.50)
After another heartbreak, New York secretary Elandra Lloyd is off to the Bahamas to visit her sister. Her sister is nowhere to be found. Instead she runs into Nassau's richest, self-made millionaire Bradley Davenport. She is lucky to have made the acquaintance with this sexy islander as she searches for her sister and her trust in the opposite sex.

Available wherever paperbacks are sold, or order direct from the Publisher. Send cover price plus 50¢ per copy for mailing and handling to Kensington Publishing Corp., Consumer Orders, or call (toll free) 888-345-BOOK, to place your order using Mastercard or Visa. Residents of New York and Tennessee must include sales tax. DO NOT SEND CASH.